P9-BJY-797

Tamsin looked at him, totally confused

He was doing it again, cutting the ground from under her feet.

"Well, anyway," she said, "that was no reason to come on to me." She felt herself flush at the memory of that embrace, and quickly continued, "It was just stage three in your softening-up process, wasn't it? Stage one, helping me with the lambing, stage two, taking me up in your balloon—just the kind of treat to turn the head of a sweet, simple kid like me."

Zak opened his mouth to interrupt, but she swept on.

"And now stage three, a kiss and a cuddle, and I'm putty in your hands." In spite of herself, there was a tremor in her voice. "I should have guessed earlier, of course— I've known all my life just what a calculating swine you are!"

RACHEL FORD was born in Coventry, descended from a long line of Warwickshire farmers. She met her husband at Birmingham University, and he is now a principal lecturer in a polytechnic school. Rachel and her husband both taught school in the West Indies for several years after their marriage, and have had fabulous holidays in Mexico, as well as unusual experiences in Venezuela and Ecuador during revolutions and coups! Their two daughters were born in England. After stints as a teacher and information guide, Rachel took up writing, which she really enjoys doing the most—first children's and girls' stories, and finally, romance novels.

Books by Rachel Ford

HARLEQUIN PRESENTS
1160—A SHADOWED LOVE
1304—LOVE'S FUGITIVE
1337—WEB OF DESIRE
1368—LORD OF THE FOREST
1402—AFFAIR IN BIARRITZ
1424—RHAPSODY OF LOVE

HARLEQUIN ROMANCE
2913—CLOUDED PARADISE
3116—LOVE'S AWAKENING

Don't miss any of our special offers. Write to us at the following address for information on our newest releases.

Harlequin Reader Service
P.O. Box 1397, Buffalo, NY 14240
Canadian address: P.O. Box 603,
Fort Erie, Ont. L2A 5X3

RACHEL FORD

man of rock

Harlequin Books

TORONTO • NEW YORK • LONDON
AMSTERDAM • PARIS • SYDNEY • HAMBURG
STOCKHOLM • ATHENS • TOKYO • MILAN
MADRID • WARSAW • BUDAPEST • AUCKLAND

If you purchased this book without a cover you should be aware
that this book is stolen property. It was reported as "unsold and
destroyed" to the publisher, and neither the author nor the
publisher has received any payment for this "stripped book."

Harlequin Presents first edition August 1992
ISBN 0-373-11479-6

Original hardcover edition published in 1990
by Mills & Boon Limited

MAN OF ROCK

Copyright © 1990 by Rachel Ford. All rights reserved.
Except for use in any review, the reproduction or utilization
of this work in whole or in part in any form by any electronic,
mechanical or other means, now known or hereafter invented,
including xerography, photocopying and recording,
or in any information storage or retrieval system, is forbidden without
the permission of the publisher, Harlequin Enterprises Limited,
225 Duncan Mill Road, Don Mills, Ontario, Canada M3B 3K9.

All the characters in this book have no existence outside the
imagination of the author and have no relation whatsoever to
anyone bearing the same name or names. They are not even
distantly inspired by any individual known or unknown to the
author, and all incidents are pure invention.

® are Trademarks registered in the United States Patent and
Trademark Office and in other countries.

Printed in U.S.A.

CHAPTER ONE

A TWIG snapped under her foot and Tamsin froze, her breath catching in her throat. But there was no reaction from the man. He continued to lean against the trunk of the tree, staring down into the fast-moving stream.

Without warning, the moon slid out from behind the bank of cloud and she hastily stepped back into the dense shadow of the oak tree just beside her. Screwing her eyes up, she peered at him once more, but he was only a vague blur, a blacker outline against the black bushes, and she would have walked right into him if he had not moved slightly, alerting her as she'd approached.

Every sense was sharpened by the darkness of the wood all round her, so that the small night sounds—one branch rasping softly against another, the last few dead leaves of winter rustling above her, a furtive movement as some tiny creature scuttled through the undergrowth—were magnified a hundred times.

In the distance a barn owl hooted, an eerie sound that made the hairs on the back of her neck prickle. But was it really an owl, or some other predatory creature of the night? One of her fellow hunters, perhaps—or the enemy? But there was no other sound, so gradually her heartbeat settled down to a steady rhythm again.

Pulling the black Balaclava further down over her face, she left the shelter of the tree and silently raced across the last few yards of open space, the grass barred with black and silver tiger stripes in the moonlight, to fetch up against the gnarled trunk of another tree.

She could see her quarry quite clearly now; his back was towards her and he was scuffing at a mossy boulder on the stream edge. The fool! He was completely off guard, obviously thinking that he was quite safe in this obscure corner of the wood. But knowing—and loving—every inch of this territory since childhood, Tamsin had tracked him down.

Surreptitiously she slid the gun from her belt, then reached into her flak jacket, brought out the bullet and slid it into the chamber. Gently nudging away another dead twig with her toe, she emerged from cover again, keeping herself sideways on to present the smallest target.

She raised her left wrist and laid the muzzle of the gun across it to steady her aim, the metal gleaming chill in the moonlight. Just for a moment, her hand wavered; he was making it too easy for her. But then she fought down that twinge of compunction, took aim again and, with a thrill wholly lethal, wholly delicious, she tightened her finger on the trigger.

In the same hair's breadth of time, though, some instinct must have finally broken through to him.

He spun round, and this reflex action took him straight into a crouching spring as he launched himself directly at her, coming in low, his right hand already raised. But he was too late; the blast caught him full on the chest.

'Bang, you're dead!' she yelled, but then, as she caught sight of the man's face, her shout of triumph died abruptly to a quaver of terror, and, hurling down her gun, she turned to flee.

But this time he was too quick for her, and she felt her right arm seized and wrenched brutally behind her back. Despite her frantic urgency to escape, she forced herself not to struggle, for it was clear that she was held in a grip that was ruthlessly professional.

'What the hell do you think you're playing at? Well?'

As she kept silent, he gave her arm a savage tweak, which all but dislocated her shoulder and made the sweat break out on her forehead. Keeping a tight hold, he swung her round to face him.

'Right. Let's have a look at you, laddie.'

With his free hand, he ripped the Balaclava away, and as Tamsin, desperate not to be recognised, wriggled in his grasp he dragged her upright and, catching hold of a handful of hair, twisted her face to his. Her sight was blurred with tears of pain, but she could see all too clearly the dye from her bullet, a crimson tide spreading across his pale blue sweater. His left cheek was splashed and his eyes, slate-grey in the moonlight, were even colder than she remembered.

'Now, who the devil are you?'

When she still did not speak, he freed her hair, and before she could shrink from his touch he roughly wiped some of the camouflage mud streaks from her cheeks and forehead.

'Good God, I don't believe it!' He was gaping down at her.

'H-hello, Zak.'

'*Tammy?* Tammy Westmacott? You little fool! What the hell are you up to?'

Finally managing to pull herself together, she replied coldly, 'I might ask the same of you. And perhaps you'd be good enough to loose my arm, before you completely break it.'

He released his grip fractionally and she pulled free, rubbing her wrist. There would no doubt be a massive bruise by tomorrow.

'I suppose you know you're trespassing,' she went on, still managing to keep a chill formality in her voice. 'Your land ends at the stream.'

'Oh, yes, I was forgetting,' he said carelessly. 'But after all, your family may have owned Luscombe for how long—four years? But we owned it for five hundred before that. Anyway,' as she glowered up at him, 'what are you going to do about it? Do some more of your pocket-sized Rambo stuff and throw me off single-handed?'

'Yes, you'd like that, wouldn't you?' she retorted. 'Give you another chance to manhandle me. Perhaps you'll completely break my arm next time.'

'I might do just that,' he said grimly. 'You don't know how lucky you are. I turn and see a figure in camouflage, gun in hand, coming for me? Honey, I was trained to break necks in that situation.'

As she looked at him uncertainly, he went on, 'And now perhaps you'll kindly tell me,' he was eyeing her combat jacket and trousers with obvious distaste, 'just why you're prancing around Luscombe Wood dressed up like Action Man.'

'Actually, I'm taking part in a war game,' she replied, in her haughtiest tone.

'A——?' He gave a snort of derisive laughter. 'Well, I suppose it's no more than I'd expect. You always were a tomboy, having problems deciding which sex you belong to.'

The casual jibe stung her and she drew herself up, scowling into his face. 'Now look here——'

'But even for you, surely it's a bit kinky, playing at soldiers out here all on your own?'

'I am *not* on my own. There's a whole group of us.'

As if in confirmation of her words, they heard what sounded like a stampede of bull elephants through the nearby undergrowth, followed by a hoarse shout of jubilation.

'Well, all right then, a whole group of you in Luscombe Wood playing at soldiers.'

'Oh, sorry,' snapped Tamsin, 'I suppose it must seem rather petty to you. I was forgetting that Zachary Trenchard is a real live soldier. Royal Marine Commandos, isn't it?'

His lips tightened. 'You're behind the times, sweetie. I—left two years ago.'

'You left?' she repeated. 'But it was your whole life—the only thing you ever cared about,' she added bitterly but, fortunately perhaps, he did not pick up her last words.

'I was invalided out,' he said, but behind the flatness of his tone she sensed the frustration and anger. 'I've been working in London.'

None of this had reached the village, she thought involuntarily. When Zak had walked out that second, final time, five years ago, he really had cut himself off from everything in his past. So in that case——

'Why have you come back now?'

'I'm visiting my father. Maybe you've heard he's ill.'

'Yes, I've heard.'

But she did not add that she had refused to allow the news that James Trenchard was confined to his bed after a stroke to touch her in the slightest. Or that the village had hashed over that final rupture between father and son many times and decided that, after the harsh words that had been said, and even, according to one of the maids at the Manor, the blow that the father had struck, Zak would never, in any circumstances, return.

'Anyway, I was on my way to see you,' he said. 'I want to talk to you.'

'Oh? Surely there's nothing for us to talk about.'

'But I think there is. You see, I have a little business proposition to put to you.'

'I'm not interested in any proposition from you— or your father,' she blurted out, but then bit her lip, somehow forcing down the naked hostility that was threatening to engulf her.

He stared at her, as though taken aback by the bitterness in her tone, but before he could reply a figure burst out into the open at the far end of the clearing, then disappeared into the night, hotly pursued by another wildly gesticulating shape.

Tamsin seized her chance. 'I-I can't talk. I have to get back to the house to organise the refreshments.'

He seemed about to argue, then shrugged. 'OK, I'll see you another time.'

'I've told you, we have nothing to say to one another. Just leave it, will you?'

Before he could reply, she swung round and started off along the narrow path.

'Hey, soldier boy.'

Reluctantly, she turned to see Zak still standing where she had left him.

'You've forgotten this.'

A moment later, her dye gun landed neatly at her feet. She snatched it up and went on down the path, his soft laugh pursuing her.

'Bye, Tamsin. See you next month.'

She stood in the gateway, waving as the battered old university minibus lurched away up the track, then slowly pushed the farmyard gate to and stood leaning against it. The students were great fun— some of her favourite clients—but sometimes, even though she was only a year or so older than most of them, she found their youthful exuberance rather hard to take.

Tonight, having been up as usual since first light, and then being roped in to make up one of the teams when they had arrived one short, she felt bone-weary in every limb. She'd wash up, then collapse into a hot bath—that was if the geyser wasn't playing up yet again.

Whatever else she did, though, she'd have to put all the cotton drill combat uniforms in soak, or they wouldn't be ready for that Young Farmers group on Saturday. She glanced down ruefully, seeing the scarlet stain on her own jacket. Usually, when she joined in a game, her intimate knowledge of every tree and bush in the wood kept her clear of being either captured or 'killed'. But tonight, as she'd made her way to the farmhouse, she'd walked straight into an enemy ambush. She'd obviously had her mind on other things. Well, one other thing, she amended grimly: Zak Trenchard.

And later, even while she'd been stirring the big pan of tomato soup, arranging the cheese and ham rolls on plates, and tending to a few real battle scars, she'd been able to think of nothing but him. Oh, damn him. Why had he come back, and, infinitely more important, what was this 'little business proposition' he wanted to put to her? Well, she'd told him clearly enough that she wanted nothing to do with him, so perhaps he'd take the hint.

She latched the gate and turned towards the house, but then, in spite of her fatigue, she stood for a few moments, letting the familiar feelings for the old building flood through her, momentarily washing away her tiredness. Wethertor Farm! The long, low house huddled into the ground, almost as though its thick granite walls and thatched roof were rooted in it, and behind she could dimly see against the night sky the rocky flank of Wethertor Hill, which for five centuries had sheltered it against the bitter north-east winds that every winter whistled down across the open expanse of Dartmoor.

Her heart was filled suddenly with a fierce, possessive love. Whatever it cost her, whatever the sacrifice, she'd never let the place go—if nothing else, she owed it to her father, and to all the shadowy generations that had gone before him. She gave a wry little smile. Tamsin Westmacott versus the rest of the world—was that how it was going to be? Very probably, she thought, as she remembered the letter she'd received from her bank manager only that morning. Oh, well, ten five-pound notes were rustling crisply in her pocket from tonight's activities, so she'd at least be able to pay the bill for those pig-nuts.

As she walked back across the yard, Joss whined softly from behind the old stable door. Whenever groups came Tamsin had to put him safely under lock and key, for, fiercely protective of her as he was, he took violent exception to her being captured or 'zapped'. Pity she hadn't had him with her tonight. If she had, Zak Trenchard might have gone back over the stream in a bit of a hurry.

She swung open the door and the large black and white collie dog leapt out at her, wagging his tail and licking her as though she'd been away for days.

But then all at once he froze, crouching on the ground, a low, menacing growl rumbling in his throat, and when she put a hand on his collar she felt the hackles standing on end.

'Shh, Joss, it's all right. They've gone.'

But he only went on growling, and as she followed the direction of his gaze, her grip tightened instinctively and her stomach muscles went into a rigid little spasm of fear.

'Who's there?'

The man had been lounging on the stone bench in the shadow of the big overhanging porch, but now he straightened up and came forward, the moonlight glinting on his face and hair. Joss's growls erupted into a volley of barks and Tamsin could barely restrain him.

She walked up the yard, clutching the struggling animal by the collar, and stood, regarding her visitor.

'How did you get in here?'

'Through the side gate, of course.' Zak gestured in the direction of the moor. 'I didn't like to interrupt—you were busy seeing off your toy soldiers.' He eyed Joss speculatively. 'That's quite a dog you've got there.'

'Yes, and I don't know how long I'll be able to hold him for,' she said, and when he made no effort to go, she added pointedly, 'He doesn't like strangers.'

But Zak only laughed. 'Strangers? Oh, come on, Tammy. I've known you since you were knee-high to an undersized gnat, so don't come the lady of the manor stuff with me.'

'No,' she retorted, 'I'll leave the *lord* of the manor stuff to you and the rest of the Trenchards!' In spite of her best intentions to show no emotion where this man was concerned, she could hear the bitterness creeping into her voice again, so she went on with a forced coolness, 'Anyway, now you're here, what do you want?'

'I told you earlier, I wanted to see you—another time. Well, this is it.'

'I'm sorry, but it'll have to wait till morning. It must be past ten, and I'm very tired.'

He scrutinised her upturned face. 'Yes, you look it.' She glanced at him sharply, but there was no trace of irony in his voice. 'But what I have to say won't take long, Tammy——'

Tammy. The old pet name, which no one outside her family—except him and Sarah—had ever used.

'My name's Tamsin,' she said coldly. 'Nobody calls me Tammy now.'

'—so if you'll just invite me in. Unless, of course, you're planning on staying out here in the yard all night.'

Very deliberately, he leaned against the granite wall of the porch and folded his arms. She glowered up at him as the short battle of wills was waged between them, then, taking her defeat as gracefully as she could, she muttered, 'All right, you'd better come in.'

Still keeping a tight hold of Joss's collar, she pushed past him to open the door which led directly into the big farmhouse kitchen, and he followed, stooping under the low lintel. She dragged Joss across to his basket beside the old Aga stove, then, as the dog stood, still regarding Zak with deep suspicion, she said through her teeth, 'It's all right, boy—*friend*.'

'I do hope so, *Tammy*.' She glared at him through her bedraggled fringe of fair hair, but said nothing. 'After all, we always were good friends, the three of us, weren't we?'

Was he totally insensitive—or was he setting out deliberately to undermine her with his seemingly casual words? The latter, probably, she decided, so she merely said, her tone expressionless, 'That was a long time ago, Zak.'

'Yes—a very long time ago.'

His voice was sombre and he was silent for a moment, as he allowed his gaze to range slowly around the kitchen, where once he had been nearly as much at home as she was. As though through his eyes, she saw the familiar, shabby yet beloved room, with its big scrubbed pine table, the enormous old dresser, loaded with the magpie array of bits of china that her mother and grandmother had collected over the years, the polished quarry tiles, the bright rag rugs. From the far corner came the slow tick of the grandfather clock which had stood in that same corner for two hundred years, one side slightly propped up because of the uneven floor, while from behind its bars the Aga fire flickered and sizzled as a log dropped.

'A long time ago,' he repeated softly, 'but nothing's changed.' Then, as though to shake himself free of the mood that had momentarily gripped him, he grinned at her. 'Not even you. What on earth were you up to, capering round the woods like a ten-year-old?'

'I told you, it was a war game. I rent Luscombe Wood out to groups who want to play. These games, they're all the rage.'

'So I've heard.' His tone was faintly ironical.

'They were students tonight—thirty of them. Or rather, twenty-nine,' she amended. 'They were short, so I made up one of the teams. I don't very often join in, of course,' she added hastily, as she caught what looked like a gleam of amusement in those cool grey eyes.

'But I bet you enjoy it when you do.' Zak eyed her up and down, taking in her old anorak, the torn jeans and muddy trainers. 'Really, Tammy, when are you going to grow up?'

She regarded him unflinchingly, determined that nothing he said would get through to her. 'Oh, I've grown up, Zak—I've had to, these last few years. But yes,' she went on rapidly, before he could interrupt, 'they make a change from the farm routine, and besides——' Now she did break off.

'Besides?' He raised his dark brows enquiringly.

'Oh, nothing.'

She had been about to say that to be in the centre of a large, boisterous group, even if it was only for two or three hours, helped assuage the loneliness she'd so often felt these last few months. But she did not say it; she did not want Zak Trenchard's pity.

All this time he had been leaning against the door-jamb. Now, though, he straightened up suddenly and, limping across the room, pulled out one of the pine chairs and let himself down heavily into it.

She watched him, covertly at first, but then, as he sat frowning down at the table, more openly. He was clearly in considerable pain, his lips clenched tightly in a thin line. How had he hurt himself? Had it been in the wood tonight, after she'd left him, stumbling over a fallen log in the darkness, perhaps?

Or was it some more serious, more lasting wound? He'd said he'd been invalided out of the Commandos, hadn't he? Tamsin's heart contracted. Zak—always so active, so physical, so overbrimming with animal vitality. However could he have borne such a blow...?

He was sitting directly under the light now, and for the first time she saw his face clearly and registered the harsh lines around his eyes and mouth. He was barely thirty, but tonight he looked much older. Only the proud set of his head on his shoulders, the arrogance that lurked around that thin mouth, remained of the boy, the young man she'd hero-worshipped for so many years. But then he lifted his hand, impatiently raking through the raven-black sweep of hair, and without warning the familiar gesture wrenched savagely at her insides.

He must have caught—though luckily not wholly understood—the look on her face, for his lips tightened again. 'Don't worry, Tam. My leg's not always this bad. It's just that I'm tired after driving down from London this evening.'

'Is that——' she hesitated, then went on, trying to pick her words delicately '—why you left the Marines?'

Grudgingly, he nodded assent.

'But how did it happen?'

'Oh, I'd been seconded to a UN peacekeeping unit in the Middle East, and some of the locals weren't too keen on having the peace kept for them.'

'I'm sorry,' was all she could trust herself to say.

'I lived,' he said curtly. 'Two of my men weren't so lucky.'

His voice was hard, but she sensed the pain beneath it and she could feel the compassion welling up in her once more. But she must not feel pity for this man—it could so easily undermine all her resolve. As she struggled with her inner feelings, though, their glances met and held.

'Tammy——' he began, but she blurted out,

'Y-you've still got some of the dye on your face.'

'Have I?' He pulled out a folded handkerchief from his trouser pocket and held it out to her. 'Wipe it off, then.'

Reluctantly, she came round the table, took it from him and, with slightly shaking hands, began rubbing at the spots of dye on his forehead. To hold him steady, she was forced to put her hand on the top of his head, and as she rested her palm on the thick, springy hair she felt again the echo of that wrenching pain. She worked in silence, conscious of the nearness of him, his thigh brushing against hers, his arm against her stomach, then as soon as she was able to she stood back.

'It's just about gone.' Without meeting his eye, she gave him back the handkerchief. 'I suppose I've ruined the sweater.'

Zak shrugged negligently. 'Think nothing of it.'

'But it wasn't really my fault, you know. You shouldn't have been there.'

He scowled irritably. 'Now don't start that again, for God's sake.'

In the corner, the clock wheezed, then struck the half-hour. Tamsin glanced at it very pointedly, but he refused to get the message. Instead he leaned forward, his elbows on the table, his chin resting on his linked fingertips, and studied her appraisingly.

'How are you managing, now that you're on your own?'

'So you've heard, have you?'

'Yes, Mrs Meadows told me about your father earlier this evening. A heart attack, wasn't it?'

'In the end, yes. At least, that's what Dr Bridges put on the death certificate,' said Tamsin, in a cold little voice.

'I'm very sorry, Tammy.'

'Are you?'

His brows went down in a slight frown. 'What's that supposed to mean?'

'Oh, nothing.'

To cover her inner turbulence, she went across to the grandfather clock. Lifting down the old brass key, she opened the glass front and began winding it methodically, trying to soothe herself with the small nightly ritual.

'And Sarah Warren. How is she?'

Her hand froze momentarily, then she forced herself to continue winding.

'I heard she got married.'

With exaggerated care, Tamsin replaced the key, then turned slowly to face him.

'And didn't you also hear that she's dead?'

CHAPTER TWO

'DEAD?' Zak stared at Tamsin, his face blank with shock. 'But when?'

'Oh—last year,' she said tonelessly. 'September.'

'Oh, Tammy, how terrible for you. You and Sarah—you were always such good friends.'

Abruptly, he pushed back his chair and crossed the room, but when he reached out to take her in his arms, she pushed him away.

'No. Don't you dare touch me!'

As she backed up against the dresser, Joss stirred in his basket and raised his head to watch them both, but Zak's arms fell back by his side.

'Look. You've obviously had a rough time of it lately—first your best friend, then your father. But what's eating you?'

'Nothing.' She bit off the word.

'Oh, come on, don't give me that,' he said angrily. 'You've been snapping my head off like an ill-tempered little vixen ever since I got here.'

'I've told you—nothing.' She looked up at him defiantly. 'What should be the matter?'

For a moment he eyed her as though tempted to catch hold of her and shake whatever it was out of her, but then he merely said, 'But what happened to Sarah? Was it an accident?'

'No. It was Mike Yeobright she married. Did your grapevine tell you that, too?'

He nodded.

'Well, they soon found that they couldn't make much of a go of farming here——' or of anything else, for that matter, thanks to you, she thought with a spurt of bitterness '—so they went out to farm in Australia, in the outback. She had a miscarriage and died before Mike could get help.' In spite of her determination to remain totally in control of herself, her voice trembled slightly. 'And that's all.'

All—except that, through your callous disregard for anyone's feelings but your own, you'd made it totally impossible for her ever to find real happiness with any other man. If ever there was a marriage on the rebound, it was hers.

Unable to meet Zak's intense gaze, her eyes strayed round the kitchen and all at once there came to her mind a cameo scene of that dreadful wedding morning. She and Sarah, facing each other in the almost identical room of the Warren family's farmhouse, she in her blue velvet bridesmaid's dress—fittingly, the wedding had been a midwinter one—and Sarah in her long white gown. The villagers said afterwards there'd never been a more beautiful bride, but behind the fragile, doll-like beauty, only Tamsin had seen the frozen heart.

Once again she heard herself desperately urging, 'You're marrying Mike, not Zak. Forget him—he's not worth it.' And when her friend had just stared at her, 'Or else you must call the whole thing off.'

But Sarah had merely given the tiniest shake of her head, which was all she could allow herself, and picked up the posy of white freesias——

'No, that's not all. That's obvious.' Zak's voice broke into her thoughts and she jerked her eyes back to him, to find that he was still regarding her closely. 'I wish you'd tell me everything, Tam. It might even help,' he added in a softer tone.

But he wasn't going to prise the whole pathetic story from her. If nothing else, she owed it to Sarah's memory—to the girl, two years older than herself, both only children, growing up on neighbouring, isolated moorland farms. Their friendship had weathered every storm since the three-year-old Tamsin, at the church playgroup, up-ended a tub of pillar-box red paint over Sarah's immaculate blonde curls and pink gingham smock dress.

After her mother's early death, Tamsin had clung to Sarah with an even fiercer loving loyalty, and over the years, as the relationship developed into a close though wholly innocent intensity, Sarah had become almost the sister she'd never had...

No. Zak must never know how much his going had annihilated her. She returned his gaze stonily.

'What is it you wanted to see me about?'

He studied her for several more long moments, but then shrugged. 'OK, have it your way. I want to buy back Wethertor Farm.'

'What?'

It was her turn to stare at him. A proposition—that was what he'd said, back in the wood. And yet how could he stand there, so calmly, as though putting just any cold-blooded business deal to her? But that was exactly what it was to him, of course—the way he viewed everything. Calculating, cold-eyed, cold-blooded.

Her mind was reeling, though, and to give herself time to think she said, 'But your father only sold it to us four years ago.'

'Yes, but he now realises that he made a mistake.'

She looked at him, her eyes narrowed. 'You mean, *someone's* persuaded him that he made a mistake.'

Zak gave a brief, mirthless laugh. 'You always were a sharp little thing, Tammy. A bit too sharp for your own good sometimes.'

'And this is one of those times, you mean?'

'Precisely.'

'But your father didn't think it was a mistake four years ago, did he, when he gave Dad the alternative—either buy, at the inflated land prices at that time, or lose the tenancy of the farm our family has held for hundreds of years.'

'Surely you've got your facts twisted,' he said coldly. 'Your father was more than happy to be given the chance to have his own farm.'

'I suppose that's the version you've been given—and the one you choose to believe. You may have been away, on and off, since you were seventeen, Zak, but you're a Trenchard, so you would see it that way, wouldn't you?'

'Not necessarily.' His voice was clipped. 'I haven't always seen eye to eye with my father, remember.'

'And I suppose he didn't tell you that the worry of keeping this place going, with a massive bank loan that Dad had been forced to take, combined with falling prices, killed him in the end?'

For a second, tears burnt her eyes. But, *I will not cry,* she told herself fiercely, and somehow forced them back.

Zak sank down into a chair and gestured to her peremptorily to sit opposite him. She hesitated, but then pulled out a chair for herself. He sat gazing at her without speaking for what seemed like several minutes and she felt herself growing increasingly ill at ease under his intense scrutiny.

But then, finally, as though having come to some decision, he said, 'Whatever the truth of it, you can't possibly manage the farm on your own.'

'I'm not on my own.'

'Oh, what help have you got, then?'

'Matthew insisted on staying on after Dad died.'

'Matt Hoskins?' His laugh grated on her. 'Good grief, girl, he's ninety if he's a day!'

Tamsin froze him across the table. 'He's seventy-three.'

'Well, there you are, then. A kid and an old man, running this place. I never took you for a fool, Tammy, but just how long do you think you can keep on like this?'

Involuntarily, her eyes strayed towards the letter that had come only that morning, still propped up against the pink china loving-cup on the dresser. He followed her gaze.

'I take it that's not a belated Valentine from your friendly bank manager.'

'Mind your own business,' she snapped, but in spite of herself her colour rose. 'Anyway,' she went on hurriedly, 'I'm not doing so much actual farming now. I sold most of Dad's flock of in-lamb ewes——' no need to let him know that the sale had been in response to the first warning shot from the bank manager just before Christmas '—but I've kept some, and I'm also running a score of pigs across in the pasture by the stream for a whole-food butcher in Exeter.'

'Pigs and a few sheep. Is that it?'

Stung by his tone, half patronising, half exasperated, she retorted, 'No, it's not. I'm diversifying. In case you don't know, people with hill farms and marginal land are actually being encouraged to do that.'

'What exactly are you up to, then?'

'Well, I'm hoping to turn the paddock over to some hard-standing for a caravan and tenting site. That will——'

'Is that wise?'

'Oh, don't worry,' she bristled angrily. 'You won't be able to see them from the Manor.'

'That's not what I meant,' he said evenly. 'A kid like you, on your own, could be in all sorts of trouble.'

'Don't keep calling me a kid!'

For God's sake, what was wrong with him? Couldn't he see that she was a grown-up woman of twenty-one? But then, looking past him, she caught sight of her reflection in the old mirror which hung on the wall opposite and, as usual, groaned inwardly.

Untidy fair hair, caught up hastily in a pony-tail, from which several strands were escaping, which she crossly tucked behind her ears ... Small face, totally devoid of make-up, upturned nose, wide mouth. Even her eyes, her best feature, large and a beautiful green like the sea, and fringed by black lashes, merely increased—she knew it, and raged frequently about it—her innocent, almost *ingénue* look.

How many times had she, in years gone by, stood in front of this same mirror, willing herself to grow tall and voluptuous like Sarah? She'd always felt so small and insignificant beside her friend, who'd been so much the belle of the village, with her long, softly curling blonde hair and huge blue eyes. When she was about seven, Tamsin had even asked her mother hopefully whether green eyes could possibly turn blue. But in the end, she'd given up the hopeless struggle and, going to the opposite extreme, had deliberately fostered her casual, tomboy image ...

She scowled at herself, then turning back to Zak said frostily, 'I am not a child, and I'm perfectly capable of running my own affairs.'

'That's a matter of opinion. A few caravans and tents through the summer—that's not going to keep you going for long. So why not be sensible and——?'

'I'm also,' she broke in determinedly, 'thinking of applying for an EC grant to plant conifers on the slopes up towards Wether Tor.'

'Are you now?' Again, she didn't at all like his tone. 'I seem to remember when we used to go out riding on the moor, the three of us——' she winced inwardly, but he did not seem to notice '—you hated conifers. Polluting the landscape, you used to say, and carry on alarming about how you'd like to chop down every one.'

'Yes, well——' She broke off abruptly. Beggars couldn't be choosers was perhaps not the wisest retort to fling at Zak just now.

He was regarding her, the ghost of a smile easing for a moment the taut lines round his mouth. 'What a fierce little thing you were.'

It wasn't fair. She couldn't fight him if he looked at her with that old indulgent tenderness in his eyes. Bitter-sweet pain filled her, and abruptly she said, 'Well, I've changed my mind, then. Sometimes people have to, you know. But that's not all. Those war games——'

'Ah, yes, those war games. Tell me about them.' He lounged back in his chair, hands in pockets.

'Well, you saw us tonight.'

'So I did. And how much do you charge those toy soldiers for running amok all over Luscombe Wood?'

Angrily, Tamsin felt herself being put on the defensive yet again. 'It depends. Tonight's group paid fifty pounds.'

'Fifty pounds?' The two front legs of his chair went down with a bang and he gave an incredulous laugh. 'You mean per head, I trust?'

'You know I don't,' she said sulkily. 'How on earth could students afford that?'

'Precisely,' he agreed drily. 'Which is why I don't aim to bother with students.'

'What do you mean?' Suspicion flared in her mind.

'Well, as you so rightly say, diversification is the name of the game. I've got plans for reorganising the Manor now that I'm taking it over.'

She stared at him, her sea-green eyes darkening in horror. 'You mean——' the words came out as though she were being slowly strangled '—you've come back to stay?'

'Of course. My father obviously isn't going to be able to run the place from now on, and so,' he smiled wryly, 'this prodigal son's come home to run it for him.'

'Oh,' was all she could manage. An absent Zak Trenchard, and no thought of his returning, had been bearable—just. But living elbow to elbow with her... Just for a second, the words almost came tumbling off her tongue, Yes, all right, I'll sell the farm to you. Anything, to give her the chance to get away from him. But then she bit them back.

'Yes,' he went on, 'we've been thinking along the same lines, you and I, Tammy. The only difference is that you're small time, and I intend to be in the Major League!'

'Major League?'

'Yes. I aim to deal with the big boys—national and multi-national companies—and set up full-scale macho days out for them.'

She gaped at him. 'Macho days? What on earth are you talking about?'

'Look.' He leaned forward across the table. 'You've heard of corporate hospitality, right? Treating your favoured clients to a day out at Wimbledon or Ascot, for instance?' She nodded slowly. 'Well, my idea is to take that one stage further and provide activity programmes where the customers actually *do* things—things they've always fantasised about but have never had the chance to try—instead of just spending the day drinking themselves legless in a marquee miles from the action.'

'What sort of things?'

'You name it, we'll lay it on. There'll be clay-pigeon shoots in the grounds. And anyone who's ever dreamed of driving a racing Jag at a hundred and twenty miles per hour, or a vintage Rolls—or an ex-Army tank—well, they'll have their chance with me. I'm putting in a planning application to take over that old wartime airfield the other side of the village and turn it into a circuit.'

'And you'll get permission, of course,' she snapped. 'Things always do go your way, don't they?'

'Not always,' he replied tightly.

Tamsin bit her lip. 'I'm sorry—I shouldn't have said that. It must have been terrible for you, having to leave the Marines.'

'Well, let's just say it wasn't the best day of my life. But anyway, yes, I think the application will go through. After all, it'll bring some much-needed money and employment to the village.'

'I suppose so.' He was right, she knew, but—— 'In that case, why do you want my land as well?'

'You've got Luscombe Wood, and Wether Tor itself.'

'The Tor? But it's just a hill with a heap of granite boulders on the top. Fine for running a few sheep——'

'Or covering with conifers,' Zak put in smoothly, but she would not rise to the bait.

'—but no use to you, surely?'

'Ah, now we come to the other side of Trenchard Enterprises.'

'And what's that?' she asked warily.

'These top corporations, they're also into participation events to sort out their executive high-fliers. Get them abseiling down Wether Tor, or set them down at midnight in the middle of unknown territory——' he gave her a sideways glance '—Luscombe Wood, for instance, pitch them against a team of ex-Commandos, and let them fight it out.'

'Oh, what high-falutin nonsense!' she exclaimed. 'It's no different from my war games!'

'The money is, I assure you.' His tone was sardonic. 'You'd be amazed what these firms are willing to pay to spot their next section heads. You start with a bunch of half a dozen men, all, on paper at least, much of a muchness, put them into this alien situation, and within an hour one of them will have emerged as leader, head and shoulders above the rest.'

Like you, you mean, Tamsin thought involuntarily, but did not say it. Instead she put in coolly, 'You really have got it all worked out, haven't you?'

He shrugged. 'I think so.'

'And I suppose you'd tell all my groups not to bother any more. They certainly wouldn't be able to afford your fancy prices.'

Unexpectedly, he grinned. 'No, let 'em all come. We can have concessionary rates for locals—the big boys can subsidise them.' He paused. 'Look, Tammy, this will bring in a much better harvest than conifers, I assure you. To put it mildly, trees are a long-term investment, and just how long can you afford to wait?'

His eyes slid meaningfully to that buff envelope on the dresser and Tamsin clenched her hands together under cover of the table. He really was a swine. How could she ever, even as a naïve, starry-eyed child, have looked up to him so?

Even if he had no feelings of guilt about his behaviour towards Sarah, didn't he at least have some recollection of her father and of how he had so often given the male companionship that the growing boy had so clearly craved but never received from his own father? And then her mother—hadn't she, in her loving, warm-hearted way, tried to fill the gap left in his life when his own mother, unable to live any longer with that demanding, domineering man, had one day simply walked out of their lives?

But no—it was useless to look for the slightest sign of softness in this rock-hard man.

'Just who do you think you are?' It burst out of her. 'You disappear for five years, then come swanning back here, thinking you can just take over people's lives. Why don't you go back to London, Zak, where you belong?'

A faint flush of anger suffused his face. 'For your information, this, as you so charmingly put it, is where I belong—at least as much as you do. Besides, I've got nothing to go back to London for. I've sold the security firm I set up when I left the forces—one of the big international companies has bought me out—and I'm using the profits to set up this new enterprise. So I'm afraid I'm going to be very much around, and that's something you're going to have to get used to.'

A *frisson* of something very like terror rippled through her. She knew from old the force of his personality, the absolute determination to get his own way, at whatever cost to anyone else. She was beginning to feel as though she were in a tiny boat heading for dangerous rapids and she'd lost the oars.

'I'm prepared to give you a fair price, of course,' he added.

'Well, that's big of you.'

'The current market value.'

'The current value!' she exclaimed hotly. 'But you know perfectly well that land prices have slumped terribly the last couple of years. My land is worth far less now than the inflated price Dad was forced to give for it.'

Zak shrugged. 'That's your problem, not mine. And anyway, it's swings and roundabouts. The house must be worth far more than he paid.'

'The house!' Tamsin leapt to her feet, her chair tumbling unnoticed to the floor, and stood staring down at him.

'Well, of course.' He might have been speaking to an unreasonable child. 'I shall want that as well. An unspoilt medieval Dartmoor longhouse. Those city men will run crazy to stay here—for a night, at least. They'll think they're going back to their roots, or something.'

She stared at him, feeling the bewilderment and anger war in her. How could he sit there so coolly, ticking off one item after another, disposing of her whole life?

'And besides,' he went on, his gaze roaming around the kitchen once more, 'we owned this place long before you did, don't forget. We were here for three hundred years at least, before moving out to the new house.'

The new house? An image flashed into Tamsin's mind of the grey stone, beautifully proportioned Georgian manor house, surrounded by the lusher pastures lower down the valley, where one Trenchard after another had lived for the last two centuries.

'Yes, and graciously made room for the peasants to take over here, I suppose.'

'Peasants?' He pounced on her hasty words. 'Is that how you see yourself, Tammy?'

'No, of course it's not,' she snapped. 'But that's the way you seem to see me. I'm in your way, spoiling your fancy schemes, so I've got to be removed, without having the slightest say in the matter.'

'Oh, but you're having your say right now.' His voice was silky smooth, but beneath it she could sense the anger uncurling itself. 'But why not be sensible? It really will be for the best, you know, for you as well as for me.'

'And just when do you want me out? Would Lady Day suit you?' She could scarcely trust her voice.

'Oh, I don't want to pressurise you, Tammy, you know that.'

He leaned back in his chair and she caught the gleam of satisfaction in his grey eyes. He really did think he'd won!

'Well, I'm sorry.' She banged both hands down on the table, setting the china mugs at the far end rattling. 'Wethertor Farm is not for sale—not one inch of it. Dad wouldn't have given up, and I'm not either. I'm the last Westmacott and——'

'Oh, don't be so ridiculous!' Zak too had jumped to his feet, and they were glaring at each other across the table. 'You make yourself sound like the last of some decrepit dynasty! You're young, you'll marry——'

'Never! I shall never marry.'

'Of course you will.'

'No, I shan't!' she repeated vehemently, her breast heaving with passion.

'For heaven's sake, Tammy, stop being so childish. You simply will not be able to cope here indefinitely. With the money I give you, you could buy yourself a modern house in the village—or move into town.'

Move into town? How could he say that? Did he really believe that she would ever, willingly, leave her beloved moors?

'You could spend some money on yourself, for a change,' he went on, his eyes raking cruelly over her. 'You weren't a bad-looking little thing in the old days, and if you treat yourself to some decent clothes, a hairdo——'

'No! Can't you get it into your arrogant head? I am not prepared to sell, and even if I were desperate to I wouldn't let you have it, Zak Trenchard, if you were the last man in England!'

'I see.' His lips were folded in a thin line. 'May I ask why?'

Did she really have to spell it out to him? That he had destroyed Sarah's life; that, despite the fact that they were lovers, and that, although there had been no formal engagement, he had talked to her of marriage so often that Sarah's whole world had revolved around him, he'd gone off without a word after that terrible quarrel with his father? Should she tell him how, the night before the wedding, sleeping at the Warrens' house, she'd lain awake, listening in anguish to her friend in the next room, sobbing inconsolably into her pillow?

'Let's just say I don't like the Trenchards,' she said steadily.

'So it comes down to personal spite, does it?'

'You could put it that way.'

'Because you've convinced yourself that my father did yours down, you're prepared to be this petty?'

Tamsin stared at him in disbelief. It obviously hadn't even occurred to him that her stubbornness could possibly have anything to do with his treatment of Sarah. He really had succeeded in wiping the whole episode from his mind, and would no doubt have been amazed—flattered even—to learn that Sarah hadn't done the same. Well, she wasn't going to disabuse him.

'If you say so,' she said tightly.

'Well, I warn you. I do not take no that easily—and, sooner or later, I always get what I want.'

'Really?' she retorted. 'But in this case, just for once, you won't.'

She saw his fists bunch, and for a moment she thought that this time he surely was going to get a hold of her. The anger, almost palpable, hung in the air between them, and, for the first time in her life, she was really afraid of him. Of course, she'd been scared of him often enough when she was a child and had done something deliberately to provoke Zak the boy, but this was different. Just for that instant, she was actually frightened of the cold-eyed man standing opposite her.

But then he crossed to the door and turned, his hand on the latch.

'I was wrong about one thing, Tamsin. You have changed. You always were a sweet-natured kid, but now you're as hard as nails.'

'Goodnight, Zak.'

She stood listening as his footsteps rang across the cobbled yard, then slowly, her legs trembling, she picked up the fallen chair and collapsed into it. Joss leapt from his basket and thrust a cold nose at her. Absently, her hand caressed his head.

'Oh, Joss, what a mess it all is.'

The dog whined in response, then, putting his front paws on her thigh, he nuzzled at her face, licking away the salt tear which was trickling down her cheek.

CHAPTER THREE

TAMSIN brushed the back of her hand across her hot forehead, then straightened her aching back with a groan of relief. Well, at least she'd got most of the seed-potatoes into the ground now; only one bag remained, then she just had to plant the summer salad crops.

She took out her penknife to slit open that final bag, then paused. She had to get everything planted, she knew that; with money so tight she'd be glad of everything she could grow, but today—— Spring had arrived. Small, fleecy clouds were chasing each other across a Mediterranean-blue sky, and directly overhead a skylark was trilling. After nearly three weeks of broken nights, she really ought to rest, but this afternoon was simply too marvellous to waste lying down indoors—or planting potatoes.

As she walked down the grass path that crossed the soft fruit area, she caught sight of a large brown toad which had crawled out from under some of last year's decaying strawberry leaves and was blinking sleepily in the sun. She stooped down to watch him, almost feeling his intense joy at being alive after such a long winter.

'I know just how you feel, my chick,' she whispered, then tickled his blunt nose with her finger before leaving him to enjoy the sunshine.

In the kitchen, she washed her hands, then changed from her mud-caked wellingtons into slightly cleaner trainers. There was really no need to lock up; no stray callers ever came all the way past the village and up the long track to the farm, but, just in case, she left Joss in the yard, regarding her mournfully through the bars of the gate until she was out of sight.

She made her way past the barn and lambing pen, where she and Matthew had spent so many hours the last few weeks, and where she would no doubt be again tonight. Only a few of the ewes had not lambed yet, but doubtless some of them were planning to tonight, almost as though they knew that she would be on her own, without even Matthew to help her.

She climbed over the stile, then followed the stream up through her pastures, where the grass was already growing blue-green and shiny. She picked a blade and chewed on it, tasting the sweetness of the juice. If this weather lasted, she'd soon be able to turn the ewes and the new lambs out here.

Her eye went up from the stream, which was tumbling downhill over its rocky bed, to the moors beyond, still brown and scorched by the savage winter winds. It was wild, rugged country, merciless at times, but in all its moods she loved it with a fierce passion, in her heart and the depths of her very being.

Ahead was the wood. Tamsin ducked under the overhanging hawthorn branches, then found a fallen tree-trunk and perched comfortably on it, idly picking off the lichen from its dry bark as she looked around her. The fat silver blobs of pussy-willow were bursting out, and below them clumps of celandines and primroses had appeared. Things had really moved on since she'd been here last. That had been the night of that moonlight encounter with Zak.

Zak. The past three weeks she had tried very hard never to think of him, with the result that she'd found herself thinking about him most of the time.

But at least their paths hadn't crossed, not directly at any rate, although she'd seen him several times. Once she'd glimpsed his unmistakable silhouette on horseback against the moors skyline; in the village one day, she had caught sight of him coming out of the Green Dragon pub with a group of tough-looking young men—presumably the ex-commandos he was planning to let loose on his city softies; and then, last week, she'd been taking a short cut along the narrow, high-banked lane that led up through the combe when, without warning, she'd found herself nose to nose with a gleaming new Range Rover.

As its driver, unseen behind the windscreen which glinted in the low afternoon sun, had shown not the slightest inclination to back up, Tamsin had been forced to reverse her battered old Land Rover down the tortuous lane, the other vehicle following her closely, its engine revving impatiently, before she finally turned into a muddy gateway. It was only when the Range Rover swept past that she had recognised the driver, as Zak raised his hand in a lazily insolent wave.

But so far, at least, he'd made no more direct or threatening moves in her direction... He'd said, though, that he wouldn't take no for an answer—not that she really needed him to tell her that. She remembered the old Zak far too clearly to doubt that sooner or later he would be back.

Well, whatever unscrupulous pressures he might be planning to bring to bear on her, he wasn't going to get his hands on this place. And yet just what was he up to? This unnerving thought *would* keep needling at her mind. 'Sooner or later, I always get what I want...' Well, sorry to disappoint you, Zachary Trenchard, but this time you won't. I shan't let you.

The sound of voices broke into her thoughts. Men's voices, laughter. Tamsin froze, listening. They were very close—surely they were in the wood?

The men did not at first notice her as she approached. They were standing in a group, six of them, engrossed in an animated discussion, and she stood for a few moments, watching them. They were strangers, all carefully dressed in regulation, pristine waxed jackets and green wellingtons, tweed trousers and sharp-edged corduroy caps. Who on earth were they? Just for a moment she hesitated, slightly diffident about accosting them, but then she caught the name Trenchard, and understood.

So this was what he was up to! He was moving in, bringing his city clients on to her land, without even bothering to obtain her permission. The hot anger was running through her, but she knew that if she was to handle this situation she had to keep it on a tight rein. She stepped forward.

'Can I help you?'

Half a dozen pairs of eyes briefly scrutinised her.

'I don't imagine so.' At the man's coolly dismissive tone, Tamsin felt her hands bunch into fists and she jammed them hard into the pockets of her denim dungarees.

'You realise that you're on private land?' Under their unfriendly regard, her voice came out higher than she had intended.

'Yes, we do, as a matter of fact.'

The man who seemed to have taken upon himself the role of spokesman for the group surveyed her from top to toe, and Tamsin began to wish, too late, that she had taken the trouble to change out of her grubby dungarees and old, rather shrunken white T-shirt.

'Though what's it to you?' he added, and the studied insolence of his tone stung her, bringing the angry colour flaring to her cheeks.

'I happen to be the owner—that's what it is to me,' she snapped.

'Oh, really?' The man gave an unpleasant laugh.

'Yes, and you are trespassing on it——'

'Oh, come now,' another of the group cut in. 'As a country girl born and bred——' somehow he made the term a sneer '—you surely know that trespassing is not a criminal offence——'

'Unless you've caused any damage.' Her eye had gone past them to the gate, set into the low stone wall that marked her boundary at this corner of the wood, and she saw that it was sagging at one end. 'Did you come through—or rather, over that gate?'

'What if we did?' the second man demanded belligerently.

'Any *country* girl could tell you that you don't climb over a gate at the latch end. You've broken the hinge.'

'Well, you shouldn't padlock it, then.'

'Actually, I keep it locked,' she was allowing herself to be carried away now on a tide of righteous anger, 'to keep out undesirables like you.'

'Now look here, you little——'

'Having problems, gentlemen?'

Zak's voice, smooth as silk, cut in and they all swung round, to see him standing on the far side of the wall. As they gazed in silence, he vaulted over it, rather stiffly, and came up to them.

Tamsin, slightly shielded from him by the men, watched him approach and in spite of herself a tremor of cold trepidation ran through her, instantly cooling her red-hot anger. Knowing him so well, she could pick up what the men were no doubt oblivious of, that behind the level voice he was furious, the dusky red standing out on his high cheekbones. He shot her one warning look, but otherwise ignored her totally, turning instead to the men.

'Are you having problems?' he repeated, but she was not going to let herself be intimidated. She wasn't a child now, to be put down by him.

'They're not the ones with the problems. *I* am. They're on my property.'

He still did not turn to her but instead, his voice clipped, he said, 'I'm sorry, gentlemen, but, technically speaking, the young lady is within her rights——' he paused fractionally '—for the time being, at least.'

Tamsin sucked in her breath in outrage. Was this barely veiled threat his idea of an apology? 'I suppose you thought it was clever to send them on to my land in the first place?' she snapped.

In three strides he was up to her and had grabbed her arm, swinging her slightly away from the men. 'OK, Tamsin, you've made your point,' he said between his teeth, and gave her arm a warning squeeze. 'Now, shut up.'

Her self-control was slipping again, under the amused smirks of their audience. They were clearly waiting for her, as an uppity female, to be put well and truly in her place.

'No, I won't, damn you!' she snarled. 'And let go of my arm!'

She tried to shake herself free, but his fingers tightened, digging into the soft flesh of her forearm, and she had to content herself with hurling at him, 'You probably told them to be sure and break my gate, too!'

The look he shot her from under his hooded lids was pure venom, but he only said, evenly, 'If there's any damage, I shall, of course, be happy to put it right.'

'You needn't bother, thanks. I can see to it myself.'

She knew she was being childish now. It was almost, she thought involuntarily, as though they had leapt back across the chasm of the years to the days when she would provocatively spar up to Zak. Asking for trouble, her mother had always warned her. And she'd always got it, too.

She wrenched herself free and stood, nursing her arm and glowering up at him, but Zak, more adept at disguising his feelings than she was, merely turned back to the men and said suavely, 'If you'll come this way, gentlemen, we'll continue our tour.'

As they made their way back towards the wall, one of the men made a remark. Tamsin did not quite catch it, but they all laughed—with one exception. Zak strode on, stony-faced, without another glance in her direction.

Joss heard him coming first. He pricked up his ears, raised his head from the rag rug where he lay in front of the Aga, and gave a low growl. Tamsin's hands, which had been kneading the bread dough as though delivering knock-out punches to someone's face, stilled, but then, as she caught sight of the familiar, tall figure, getting down from the Range Rover and striding across the yard—as if he already owned it, she thought resentfully—she hastily began again.

When she had returned to the farmhouse, an hour previously, she had begun making the bread as a kind of soothing ritual, and the therapy had been working—until now, that was. She heard Zak's footsteps ring on the stone floor of the porch and, in spite of herself, jumped nervously as the kitchen door flew open. From out of the corner of her eye, she saw Joss leap to his feet.

Oh, bite him, Joss, she urged inwardly, tear him in half! But the dog merely pushed his nose against Zak's hand in a joyful welcome. Well, after all, she was the one who had assured Joss that he was a friend, so she could hardly hold this act of treachery against him now.

She, though, refused to look up, only contenting herself by remarking sweetly to the dough, 'Do come in.'

From under her lashes she saw Zak advance across the room and stand facing her over the table.

'Just what the hell did you think you were up to back there?'

She could hear him breathing deeply. He was clearly still very angry, and to give herself time to gather herself for a counter attack, she asked, 'In what way?'

'You know bloody well in what way!'

For the first time, she looked up to meet the furious grey eyes. 'Well, I was seeing those charming friends of yours off my land, if that's what you mean.'

'They are not friends of mine,' he said coldly. 'They're prospective clients—or at least, they were.'

'Oh, so those are the kind of people you choose to do business with.' She knew it was dangerous, deliberately setting out to needle Zak like this, but she had to stand up to him.

'I can't afford to be choosy who I do business with—any more than you can,' he added meaningfully.

'I suppose you thought if you could once get them on to my property——'

'For your information, I did not take them into the wood deliberately. I was called up to the house to take an urgent phone call, and they wandered off on their own.'

'Who were they, anyway?'

'They're the representatives from some of the companies I've been dealing with. I was taking them on a recce, showing them the kind of facilities we can lay on for them.'

'Including Luscombe Wood, you mean?'

His lips tightened. 'Don't start that again. I've got a good mind, anyway, to take you over my knee and give you a good hiding. It wouldn't be the first time.'

'No, but it would certainly be the last. Don't you dare touch me!'

Tamsin tensed, half afraid that he really would seize her, but he only went on, 'You realise that you've almost certainly lost me my first six commissions through your juvenile behaviour?'

'Good.' She slapped the dough down on to the table and scowled defiantly across at him.

'They're on their way up to Herefordshire, where they're looking over another activity outfit, and I don't think, somehow, that they'll be back. No doubt the natives are rather more welcoming up there.'

'Oh, really?' she said pertly. But all at once, an immense weariness was settling on her, leaving her no energy any longer for this pointless bickering. With the back of her hand she brushed away a strand of hair that had flopped forward over her cheek. 'Look, Zak, if that's all you came to say, I've got work to do. In case you haven't noticed, I'm in the middle of making bread.'

'That's another thing.' He leaned against the table, watching her as she dropped the ball of dough back into the mixing bowl. 'This is all too much for you. Why not admit it? You're even having to make your own bread, when there's a perfectly good baker in the village.'

'I happen to enjoy it.'

'Maybe. Or maybe you're trying to prove something.'

'Right now, I'm trying to prove this bread,' she said pointedly, but he ignored her riposte.

'You look absolutely out on your pins. Do you know that? And you're so much thinner than you used to be.' She felt his gaze skim unflatteringly over her figure. 'In fact, you look absolutely terrible.'

'Well, thank you,' she said tightly. 'All compliments gratefully received.'

She flashed him a hostile glance, but he just shook his head.

'I wouldn't waste my time paying you compliments I didn't mean, Tammy. We know each other too well for that.'

A tiny smile flickered across his lips and, without warning, a feeling of intense sadness engulfed her. She'd thought she'd known him, all those years ago, hadn't she? Until he'd shown himself for what he really was.

'Mind you, it doesn't help to have flour all over your face.'

Before she could jerk back, he had leaned forward and with his little finger gently brushed across her cheek. It was a light enough touch, yet it set her skin tingling and she could only stare at him wordlessly.

'And you're still set on hanging on to your land?' His voice was just a shade too casual and she shook herself free from that momentary spell.

'Of course.'

'Look, Tammy. Taking that group round today, it showed even more clearly how stupid it is for you to cling on to Luscombe Wood. It's just not logical.'

'What's logic got to do with it?' she flared.

'Obviously nothing, as far as you're concerned. But can't you see how the wood cuts a wedge right through the area I want to use?'

'Well, it's a pity your father didn't think of that before he forced Dad into buying it.'

'So you're determined to make life difficult for me, out of some misplaced sense of loyalty for your father. He wouldn't thank you for that, I'm sure.

And he wouldn't want you to kill yourself with overwork in the process, either.'

'Oh, what nonsense! All right, maybe I'm over-doing it a bit at the moment, but by the weekend the lambing should be over——'

'And you're doing all that on your own, I suppose.'

'Of course not. I've done a split shift with Matthew every night, at least, until——'

She broke off abruptly. She certainly wasn't going to admit that tonight, for the first time, she really would be alone. She'd only get a patronising 'And how do you reckon you'll manage?' if she did.

'Until?' he prompted.

'Oh, until the lambing's finished, of course.'

He was regarding her with a mixture of anger and exasperation and even, perhaps, just a glint of reluctant admiration.

'You're a tough little thing, Tammy, I'll give you that. Compared with you, Sarah——'

'What about Sarah?' Her voice sharpened.

'Well, she was a lovely girl, but she was very—well, soft.'

'You should know,' she blurted out.

'And what precisely do you mean by that?'

He was frowning at her, and something in that frown held her back from all the things that she wanted to fling at him, so that, instead, she only shrugged and said, 'Well, you knew her, didn't you?'

She looked across at him steadily, then picked up the bowl, slid it inside a polythene bag and put it

into the warm compartment of the Aga. Gathering
up the dirty utensils, she began stacking them in
the sink, then, keeping her back turned to him, went
on,

'There's nothing more to be said. I'm not prepared to hand over Wethertor Farm to you—that's
final, and you may as well accept it.'

Deliberately, she turned on the tap and heard,
above the gush of water, the brief, muttered ob-
scenity, the sharp thump as Zak smacked his balled
fist hard into his other palm, and then, finally, the
slam of the kitchen door.

Tamsin shivered as an icy draught curled round her,
numbing her from the knees down. Easing herself
up stiffly from the large bale of hay she had been
perched on, she went across to the barn door.

She put her hand on the latch to close it more
tightly, but then instead pushed it open. The
beautiful spring day had turned into a cold, clear
night. Overhead, a million star points glittered like
chips of ice, while the cobbled yard gleamed blue-
white under the full moon. Somewhere far out
beyond Wether Tor, a vixen called, the eerie high-
pitched scream prickling the hairs on her neck, and
then she heard Joss's answering bark from his bed
in the old stable.

She pulled the barn door to, then, wrapping the
tartan rug round herself and snuggling down into
her old quilted parka, she settled herself on the hay
bale again, her back against another, her head on
her arms.

Across the other side of the barn, the four ewes which, with Joss's help, she had brought in from the home field at dusk stood in an uneasy little huddle. They were watching her, their eyes reflecting yellow in the circle of light cast by the two hurricane lamps she had strung from the nails in the beam. But nothing else was happening; certainly, none of them seemed in imminent danger of going into labour.

Tamsin smothered yet another huge, jaw-cracking yawn and eyed them consideringly. Maybe she'd been mistaken, in which case she might as well leave them to it and go to bed. Bed. Closing her eyes, she thought yearningly of that hot-water bottle she'd slipped in to warm the sheets.

Should she risk it? No, definitely not. Her ewes obviously hadn't been paying attention when the elderly sheep farmer the other side of Luscombe had assured her that lambs liked to be born with the sun on their faces. Every one of them, so far, had seemed grimly determined to give birth during the hours of darkness.

When lambing had begun nearly three weeks earlier, she had resolutely stayed here in the barn until midnight each night, then left the ewes to fend for themselves. But since one terrible dawn, when she'd come in to discover two pathetic little corpses and the mother in urgent need of the vet, she and Matthew had shared the work each night—at least, until tonight.

From across the yard there came a muffled bark. Joss, perhaps made restive by that vixen prowling out on the moors... Then footsteps were coming across the yard, and as she lifted her head, frowning, half puzzled, half fearful, the barn door was dragged open, its jagged edge grating harshly on the cobbles, and a man's figure, black against the moonlight, was outlined in the doorway.

CHAPTER FOUR

As TAMSIN gaped at him, Zak closed the door carefully behind him. He was wearing a bulky pale cream sheepskin jacket, and his features were shadowed by the brim of a corduroy cap. Outlined in the circle of lamplight, he looked very large and very intimidating, but something more than that seemed to emanate from him as he advanced on her—something that made her whole body tense and sent a shiver through her as he came and stood over her.

She stared up at him wordlessly, but then finally roused herself, struggling to combat the subversive emotions that had swept through her.

'Oh, God, what do you want now?' It was almost a groan; she was so exhausted that momentarily she was seeing double—two Zak Trenchards, as if one wasn't more than enough. 'If you've come to try to bully me into selling the farm again, you can just——'

'Of course I haven't, you little idiot.' She felt rather than saw the scowl. 'I'm much too attached to my bed, I assure you, to actively *want* to spend the night in a freezing cold barn arguing the toss with a stubborn little shrew like you, Tamsin Westmacott.'

'Spend the night? Wh-what on earth do you mean?' She was almost squeaking.

'What I say.'

For the first time, as he dropped them down on to the bale beside her, she registered that he had been carrying a folded rug and a large wicker box. As he straightened up, he caught her horrified expression and laughed softly, his eyes and teeth gleaming in the lamplight. To Tamsin, there was something almost wolf-like in the smile.

'I've come to help you.'

'I——' She swallowed down the obstruction in her throat. 'I don't need any help—thank you all the same,' she added, very politely. 'So there's absolutely no need for you to stay.'

'Sorry, but I am. You may be stupid enough to think you can manage on your own. You may even have persuaded Matt Hoskins that you can——'

'How did you know?' she demanded.

'Well, not from anything you said this afternoon, I assure you, my sweet.' Tamsin winced inwardly at the memory of their last encounter. 'You were caginess itself. But I was driving through the village and just happened to see Matt getting into his son-in-law's car, with an overnight case——'

'And, of course, you couldn't drive on, minding your own business——'

'—and he told me that you'd insisted that he should go down to Penzance to see his new grandchild. Swore blind you'd be all right, he said—when any fool knows that lambing is a two-man business.'

'Well, it's only for one night,' Tamsin replied, a shade sulkily. He was already managing to put her on the defensive again. 'He's an old man——'

'Just what I've been telling you.'

'——and he's waited a long time for this first grandchild, so I——'

'So you assured him you could manage. Well, I can tell you he's gone off a lot happier now he knows I'm spending the night here with you.'

Full-blown panic was flaring in her. She couldn't possibly spend an entire night with Zak, not after all the terrible things they'd hurled at each other just a few hours previously.

'No, Zak,' she almost pleaded. 'I'll be all right— I know I shall.'

'Oh, be quiet, will you?' he said, fairly amicably, though. 'I know at least as much about lambing as you do. I helped your father often enough—or have you forgotten?'

No, she hadn't forgotten. Zak at sixteen—in this very barn...'Come on, Tammy, catch hold. No, you idiot—here...' Zak, beside her now in the flickering lamplight, his grey eyes momentarily filled with the boyish enthusiasm which had so often lit them, before the hardness, the cynicism had taken him over...

Reluctantly she nodded, then watched as he dragged across another couple of bales.

'And then I had that time in New Zealand working on a sheep station, remember?'

Yes, of course...Tamsin sat thinking of the wilful boy who, having passed all his exams with no apparent effort, had, to his father's baffled fury, simply dropped out of school at seventeen and left home.

'You went to the States first, didn't you?' she asked, although she remembered well enough how she and Sarah had listened wide-eyed to his stories of his adventures as a casual farmhand following the grain harvest right up to the Canadian border.

'That's right. And then I came back home again, to try and do my dutiful son bit.'

'But you couldn't stay.' Tamsin's voice was barely a whisper.

He grimaced. 'No, I suppose I just hadn't got the wanderlust out of my system. I still wanted action, excitement, danger, so I joined the Army— and got rather more of all three than I'd bargained for.'

He dropped down on to the bales alongside her, stretching his long legs out in front of him. 'Anyway, that's all past history now—water under a good many bridges.'

And Sarah's just one of those bridges, I suppose. The words almost leapt from her, but just in time she bit them back. This was neither the time nor the place for another confrontation.

'How's the lambing gone so far?'

'Oh, pretty well.' With relief, she refocused her mind to answer him. 'I lost two lambs, but we've had one set of triplets, and plenty of twins, of course. These ewes are almost the last. I brought them in because I thought they were ready to lamb, but I'm——'

'You mean, like that one?'

Zak jerked his head in the direction of one of the sheep and Tamsin saw that it was pawing the ground restlessly and turning round and round in small circles. At the telltale signs, she leapt to her feet, but he was already peeling off his jacket and dropping it on to the bale.

In the event, though, the ewe produced her lamb with such swift efficiency that no help was needed. Zak gently held the little creature while Tamsin wiped the mucus from its tiny black muzzle and white fleece, then they watched as it hauled itself to its feet and tottered shakily across to its mother. As she nuzzled at it, their eyes met and they shared a silent smile. The miracle of birth. No matter how often Tamsin witnessed it, it never failed to move her immensely.

'Well, you've got a good sturdy one there.' Zak got to his feet. 'You know, I have a feeling it's going to be quite a long night. Let's have something to eat.'

As Tamsin watched, he scrubbed his hands in the bucket of water that stood ready nearby, then flipped open the wicker basket, lifted out a wide-mouth vacuum jar and poured soup into two bright red pottery mugs. He held one out to her.

'Here, get this down you. You look like a little skinned rabbit.'

As she hesitated, he thrust it at her impatiently. 'Go on, it's minestrone. I seem to remember that was always your favourite.'

'I—well, thank you,' she said, rather awkwardly, and took the mug, cradling it in her frozen fingers, inhaling the mouthwatering fragrance.

'Fancy a pasty?' He was reaching into the basket again.

'Oh, no, it's all right,' she said hastily, as he unwrapped the silver foil to reveal two ovals of rich golden pastry. They looked absolutely delicious—but it suddenly seemed vital to her that she shouldn't allow herself to become even more beholden to him than she already was tonight.

'I've got some cheese sandwiches,' she went on. 'Er—would you like one? They've got chutney in them.'

'Cheese and chutney?' From across the bale he flashed her a sudden, totally disarming grin. 'Yes, please—I can't resist them.'

She passed him one and he took a bite. 'Mmm, wonderful. And home-made bread. Is this what you were baking earlier?'

'Oh, no, I made this a couple of days ago.' No need to tell him that this afternoon's batch had been a total disaster: pale, leaden lumps—the results, she'd told herself angrily as she dumped them in the waste bin, of being distracted by his arrival and their angry words.

She leaned back, sipping the scalding soup and feeling it warm her all the way down before finally settling itself into a comforting band across her stomach. Surreptitiously, she eyed Zak over the rim of her mug as he took another bite of his sandwich. She just couldn't understand him, couldn't make him out at all. The two of them were engaged in a life-and-death struggle for Wethertor Farm, and yet here he was, prepared to spend a long, exhausting night in a freezing barn, helping his arch-enemy produce the very lambs which would help her keep the farm out of his grip.

Tamsin frowned, staring down at the toes of her trainers. It was all very puzzling—especially as he had never seemed particularly kind-hearted or over-concerned for other people's well-being. She only had to think of his behaviour towards Sarah to be reminded of that.

Her lips tightened and abruptly she lifted her gaze, to find his grey eyes fixed on her, an enigmatic look in them which disturbed her even further, so that she blurted out, 'Just why are you helping me like this?'

He shrugged. 'Don't ask me. Let's just put it down to auld lang syne, shall we?'

'Auld lang syne?'

'Old times' sake, then. After all, we used to be pretty close, didn't we, Tammy?' She stirred uncomfortably. 'And you're a plucky little thing, even if you are a bone-headed, cussed little madam.'

Hmm. Tamsin gave him a long look, but tonight she wasn't going to quarrel with him if she could help it. Instead, she took another sip of her soup.

'This is lovely,' she said, rather stiffly. 'Did you make it?'

He pulled a face. 'Heavens, no. Mrs Meadows prepared it for me. I may be thoroughly domesticated, but I'm not up to minestrone soup standard yet, I'm afraid.'

She could not resist an incredulous laugh. 'You—domesticated? You're about as domesticated as——' she glanced around her for inspiration '—as the wildcat that hangs around here killing the rats.'

'A wildcat? Well, I may have handled a few rats in my time, but watch it, young lady.' Zak growled mock-threateningly. 'More soup?'

'No, thanks. At least—perhaps later.'

She leaned her head back, so that the hay tickled her neck, and studied him once more. He was holding his mug between his hands, absently swirling the remnants of soup around and frowning down into it. The pale yellow light from the hurricane lamps gleamed on the top of his head, giving each springy black hair a gilt-tipped edge and softening the hard lines of his face, dusting them with gold.

In the background, the light melted and merged into the black shadows of the barn, where the sheep moved softly, but within the lamp-glow the two of them seemed to be caught up in a small circle of intimacy.

Very deep inside her, something so nebulous that she could not put a name to it—a feeling, a sensation—stirred into life. Just for a moment, intense pain and intense joy flowered in her simultaneously, then, without warning, ridiculous tears were stinging her eyes. Terrified that Zak would see them, and laugh at her as a silly little fool, she turned her head sharply away and closed her eyes.

'Look, you're all in, Tam. Why don't you go to bed?'

Her eyes flew open, to see Zak leaning towards her. He put out his hand to lift her, but, still bewildered by that strange, disorientating sensation, she jerked away from him. His face at once took on that chill, forbidding mask and he too drew back instantly.

'I can manage here quite well, you know,' he said coldly.

'No,' she replied obstinately. 'They're my responsibility, and I'm not going to leave them.'

And, even as she spoke, she saw that another of the ewes was in labour. As they stood watching, though, it quickly became very obvious that this was not going to be anything like as straightforward a lambing as the last.

For over an hour they crouched by the sheep, sharing its growing distress as it strained and struggled, but to no effect, until at last Tamsin sat back on her heels in the straw and looked up at Zak.

'I can't stand this,' she whispered shakily. 'It's her first time—she'll never make it. I'll go and phone the vet.' Though goodness knew what a hole that would make in her tight monthly budget.

Many farmers, she knew—including her father— rarely bothered to call on expensive professional help for a ewe or a lamb. Cows and calves were valuable, but sheep were expendable. She, though, was always too upset by the sight of any animal suffering to be able to bear it for very long.

But even as she scrambled stiffly to her feet, Zak exclaimed urgently, 'Hang on—something's happening! Oh, damn, damn, damn! I think the head's coming first.'

'That settles it. I'll go and ring.'

'*No*—wait,' he said in a fierce undertone, as he too got to his feet. 'Let me have a go.' As she gazed at him, he went on, 'Look, you've got nothing to lose. By the time the vet gets here, it'll almost certainly be too late. Trust me.'

Tamsin hesitated, gnawing her lip indecisively, then nodded. 'All right.'

Zak was already dragging off his navy polo sweater. He threw it on to the bale, followed by his white shirt, then he thrust his hands into the bucket of water. As Tamsin stared tensely at him, he rubbed the wet tablet of soap all over his hands and arms, then straightened up and came back across to her as she knelt by the ewe.

For a moment he looked down at her, his eyes gleaming silver-grey in the lamplight, a little half-smile playing round his mouth, then he came down on his haunches beside her.

'Now, stop it. No howling, or I'll send you back to the house.' And before she could draw back out of range, he had dropped a kiss lightly on the end of her nose.

Tamsin gaped at him blankly, stunned into silence by that totally unexpected kiss, but then she found enough voice to say, 'I'm not crying,' even as she surreptitiously wiped away a tear.

But Zak only grunted, as though he barely heard her. Frowning now in absolute concentration, his head on the arm which lay across the animal's back, black hair against white fleece, he waited for the ewe to stop straining. When at last, exhausted, she was still he immediately pushed in his hand and gave a long, slow thrust, his breath quickening with the effort.

At last he withdrew his hand and Tamsin looked questioningly at him.

'I think I've managed to turn its legs forward,' he whispered softly. 'But it's a hell of a big lamb for her to throw. We'll still lose it if we're not careful. Look—get me a rope, a cord, anything.'

Leaping to her feet, she snatched up the coiled length of thin rope which always hung in the barn. Zak grabbed it from her, measured a length, then took a penknife from his pocket, cut it and ran it through the soapy water between his fingers.

'Right,' he said curtly, 'I shall want some leverage. Help me lift her over to the wall. This side, so I can use my good leg as a brace.'

He had taken all control out of her hands, but Tamsin could only be grateful. Between them they caught hold of the ewe, now apparently too far gone to protest, and carried her across to the wall, where they carefully laid her down. Zak waited tensely, the cord between his fingers, one hand on her abdomen, then swiftly and efficiently, between the waves of rhythm from her uterus, he slid in his hand, taking in one end of the rope.

His hair was flopping over his face, the perspiration was glistening on his brow, and all at once Tamsin ached to reach across and wipe it off. But just as her fingers began to curl, he brought out his hand and wiped the sweat away himself with his clean forearm.

'Take hold of her,' he commanded, 'and when I say now, pull away from me, long and hard. Wait— wait——' they were both watching the ewe intently '—*now*!'

As she pulled, he braced himself against the wall and tugged both ends of the cord.

'OK. Rest.' He was panting with the effort, but he grinned reassuringly across at her. 'We'll do it, I promise. Ready? Now—pull again.'

And several heaves later, the lamb—a black one—was lying inert on the straw-covered floor.

Tamsin knelt and rubbed it all over, cleaning the mucus away, but still it lay, a limp bundle of legs and tiny hoofs. Cursing softly, Zak picked it up; he laid it across his knees and began blowing hard down its throat, but still there was not the least flicker of life.

'Oh, give in, Zak. It's dead.' After the exhilaration of working with him, bringing out the lamb, the disappointment was almost too much.

'Shut up!' he almost snarled at her. 'I'm darned if I will. I don't give in that easily.'

He rolled the lamb over and began massaging its heart, round and round, with probing, methodical hands. Tamsin, just behind him, stared at the slender fingers, so strong yet so sensitive, as they worked. His back muscles were moving rhythmically against the silky skin—deeply tanned except where, low down, his black jeans had pulled away from his belt in his exertions, and there was a narrow ribbon of paler flesh where the tan ended abruptly.

She stared in fascination at that pale skin which, in her imagination, ran down over the slim, taut haunches and round to his stomach. As her pulses began to beat slow and torpid, the blood filling her veins, her throat tightened and she swallowed.

There was the faintest sound, more like the mew of a new-born kitten, followed by a miniature sneeze, and the lamb stirred into life.

'We've done it!'

Setting down the small, coal-black bundle, Zak turned, laughing up at her triumphantly, then without warning leapt to his feet and snatched her up into his arms, whirling her round and round until the barn reeled around her. But then, as she clung to him helplessly, the laugh faded as suddenly as it had appeared and he untwined her clutching fingers from his grasp to stand her back, unsteadily, on her feet.

Just for a moment he stared down at her, frowning as though in puzzlement, but then he said brusquely, 'You've got a good strong one here. Do you want to give it to the ewe?'

Without speaking, Tamsin carefully picked up the lamb, set it alongside the mother to be nuzzled and licked all over, and finally, as it began suckling, fetched a handful of concentrates for the ewe.

But all the time, as she performed the mechanical tasks, her body was prickling all over as though with the first symptoms of flu, and her mind was racing round and round in feverish circles. She was still dizzy from the effects of that sudden, totally unexpected flash of boyish exuberance, of course, but even before that—— What on earth had come over her, this feeling that had swept through her, gripping her so fiercely in its intensity? Surely—her eyes darkened at the appalling thought—surely she wasn't in for a second bout of the teenage crush she'd had on Zak all those years ago?

No, she told herself fiercely, it can't be. All right, she'd always adored him when she was a kid, following him around like a besotted puppy; and then, later, she'd fancied him something rotten—though that had been a bitter-sweet secret she'd hugged to herself always.

But now, after all that had happened, it couldn't possibly be that. No—it was simply seeing him just now, stripped to the waist like that, he'd looked again as if he was about to leap into that moorland pool where they used to bathe together, and, just for a moment, her mind had been playing tricks on her, awakening long-buried memories that were far better left buried. That was all it was—that was all she must allow it to be.

CHAPTER FIVE

'WELL, we did it.'

Zak had been drying his hands on the towel; now he sauntered across to Tamsin and draped one bare arm across her shoulders. The casual, friendly gesture made her heart ache. She hadn't been the only one to be affected by their struggle together to save the lamb. He too seemed to have gone back momentarily to that time when, for his part at least, their relationship had been carefree, uncomplicated.

'No—you did it, Zak. Thank you.' She ducked away from his arm, shying from all contact with that beautifully moulded muscular torso, yet hating the frown which darkened his eyes. 'I'm really grateful. I'm—I'm glad you were here,' she added simply.

'Oh,' he shrugged, 'glad I could help.' He shot her a crooked little smile and jerked his thumb in the direction of the lamb. 'After all, one black sheep should always help another.'

Tamsin smiled rather uncertainly, then said, 'Er—I've got a flask of coffee. Would you like some?'

'Yes, please.'

The careful politeness filled her with a huge sadness. In all the years they'd known one another, through all the squabbles and fights, they'd always been so open with one another, hurling insults one minute and, next instant, making up with equal gusto. Now, even after that brief, shared exhilaration, that unbridgeable fissure had formed between them again and they were reduced to a cool formality, which was, just at this moment, even more unbearable than when they were engaged in furious, open hostility.

She busied herself with the coffee, out of the corner of her eye aware of Zak pulling on his shirt, tucking it into his jeans, then tugging on his sweater.

'Black or white?'

'Black, please—and have some of this in it.' He leaned across to his jacket and took out a silver hip flask.

'What is it?'

'Rum.'

'Oh, no, thank you.'

Hastily she made to move her plastic cup back out of reach, but he caught hold of her wrist.

'Just a drop,' he said firmly. 'If you feel anything like me, you could do with it. It'll keep out the cold.' And before she could protest, he had poured in a generous slurp.

As they sat down once more on the bales, he winced slightly and eased his left leg.

'Does—does it hurt all the time?' The words were out before she could hold them back.

'No.' He seemed to be inclined to leave it at that, but then added, 'Only when I've been overdoing it. I put in a lot of physio on it—building up the muscles and so on.'

'Oh.'

Tamsin sipped cautiously at her coffee. She could certainly taste the rum, but Zak had been right. Just this once, she was glad of its warming potency. It might even help to keep her awake through the rest of the night...

'Wake up, Tammy!'

'Mmm?'

'I said wake up.'

'I'm not asleep,' she mumbled.

'No?' Zak's voice was a soft murmur in her ear. 'Then why have you been using my shoulder as a pillow for the past two hours?'

'What?'

Tamsin's eyes flicked open and she jerked her head away from him as though his body were burning hot.

'What's the time?' She looked around her, bleary-eyed.

Pulling back the cuff of his jacket, he held his wrist watch up into a shaft of pale daylight coming in through a chink in the barn door.

'Nearly six. I think you can go back to the house now.'

'But what about the other two ewes?' She managed to focus on the corner where the two remaining prospective mothers still stood. 'Have they lambed yet?'

'No—and I think we can safely leave them for a while. So come on.'

Stiffly, he stood up then, reaching down, took Tamsin's arms and pulled her to her feet. Still too befuddled to argue, she allowed herself to be led out of the barn and across to the house, where Zak steered her into the kitchen, closed the door, then turned her to face him.

'Get off to bed. You look all in.'

It was true; the accumulated fatigue of days and weeks that had been snapping at her heels had finally caught up with her—and now she had the added burden of those tumultuous reawakened feelings to contend with. But to let him see her creeping off to bed would be a sign of weakness, and Tamsin Westmacott was not weak.

'No, I'm all right,' she insisted. 'I-I'll get us some breakfast.' She would feel much happier if he went, before she betrayed to him any hint of her inner turmoil, but it was the least she could do after all the help he'd given her. 'I left the porridge in the oven—there's plenty for two.'

Zak gave an exasperated sigh. 'Of all the stubborn little——! You're cross-eyed with exhaustion, but all right, we'll compromise. You will go and have a bath—that's if you can keep your eyes open long enough to find the taps—and I'll have a bit of a scrub-up at the sink here, then we'll have breakfast. And no more arguments——' his dark brows came down in a warning scowl '—unless you want me to carry you upstairs and put you in the bath myself.'

She stared at him for one more second, trying to whip up defiance, then fled.

* * *

The bathwater was cooling. Tamsin stirred it round with her big toe to release the last of the fragrance from some of the precious Christmas gardenia bath oil, then reluctantly lay back. At first, the deliciously warm scented water had blotted out everything except sheer physical pleasure, but now she could no longer keep at bay the thoughts that were swarming into her mind.

Back there in the barn, she'd convinced herself that that fleeting spasm of feeling was no more than a sudden, totally unexpected renewal of her schoolgirl crush on Zak, but now, as she unwillingly relived that moment, she was forced to confront the truth. It was more, far more than that. What she had felt was no mere left-over adolescent hero-worship, but fully-fledged sexual desire.

As she'd watched him with the lamb, his naked torso gleaming in the lamplight, her whole body had ached to feel the touch of those probing, delicate fingers on her skin, had yearned for him to take her in his arms and hold her to him, as tenderly as he was holding that fragile little creature...

She hauled herself out of the bath, but even as she began scrubbing herself fiercely with a towel she caught sight of her reflection in the misty mirror. Half fearful of what she would see, she wiped the cold glass and, staring into it, saw, as her heartbeat quickened, a new secret self—the wide sea-green eyes dark with this new awareness, and the softly curving mouth, lips half parted as though in eager anticipation of—of what?

Furious, she dragged a corner of the towel across the mirror, smearing that treacherous reflection. This was madness, utter madness. How on earth could she hope to fight Zak, to hold on to what was rightfully hers, feeling this way about him? And what about Sarah? The thought leapt into her mind, displacing all her other fears. Surely to be so weak as to feel this way, however fleetingly, was the worst of betrayals of Sarah's memory?

One thing was for sure. Downstairs, she would have to be even more on her guard. Zak knew her far too well for him to remain unaware for long of these terrifying emotions that were washing through her, but if she could just act out a part now, then, by the time they next met up, she would have herself well under control again.

'Tammy!' Zak's voice came from the foot of the stairs.

'Y-yes?'

'Can you come down? You're needed.'

'I shan't be long——'

'No—now.'

What had happened? Surely he hadn't let the porridge boil over? She hesitated a moment, but then pulled on her ancient blue candlewick dressing-gown and hurried downstairs.

She had opened the kitchen door before she realised that Zak was not alone, and then it was too late to retreat. He was talking to Jack Beasley, the middle-aged postman who covered this huge rural post round in his van. Both men turned to look at

her as she came slowly in, and Tamsin was dreadfully aware that, with her horrified face, now no
doubt a deep scarlet, her hair tumbled in disarray,
and above all the dressing-gown, she looked the very
image of guilt. Well, she just had to brazen it out,
with Zak's help.

'Morning, Jack. You're early.' Giving him a
brilliant smile, she advanced into the room.

'Morning, Tamsin.' Surely she wasn't imagining
that behind his usual greeting there was a hint of
'Hello, hello, who's been a naughty girl, then?'
which set her teeth on edge. 'Been a long night, has
it?' he enquired blandly.

She expected Zak to leap into action, but he was
lolling back in his chair, hands in pockets.

'Yes, it has, actually,' she said, with just a hint
of cool reproof. 'Matthew was away, and Mr
Trenchard very kindly offered to help me with the
lambing.'

She glanced across at Zak for confirmation, but
to her horror saw that he was lounging even further
back in his chair, with clearly not the slightest intention of helping her out. How could he? She shot
him a sizzler of a look, then her eyes flicked back
to Jack, to see him avidly devouring every nuance.

'I was really glad he was here. We had one very
difficult birth.' She knew she was babbling, but
could not stop. 'I'd have lost it if he hadn't been
here.'

'Good, good.' The postman was poker-faced, and
she thought, Oh, God, he doesn't believe me.

'I'll get you your cup of tea,' she said coldly.

'Oh, no. Mustn't disturb you.' Disturb you? It must be the first time in living memory that Jack Beasley had refused a cup of tea. 'If you'll just sign for this packet—recorded delivery. Your next batch of oral vaccines, I shouldn't wonder,' he added, then handed her the form, together with a nub of pencil, and she bent over the table to screen her hot face.

'Right. Thank you, Jack.'

'Thanks, Tamsin. 'Bye, Mr Trenchard.'

She stood motionless as he carefully closed the door behind him, then swung round on Zak.

'Well, thanks very much.'

'What for?'

'You know perfectly well what for. Zak Trenchard? Oh, yes, he was there at seven o'clock this morning, getting the breakfast. Quite at home, he was. And Tamsin, she was still in her *dressing-gown*. Oh, God.' She shuddered at the conversations which would be taking place at every farm and cottage on the postman's round.

'Sit down and don't be so silly.'

'*Silly?*' Her voice rose half an octave. 'My reputation is ruined, you realise that?'

'Oh, Tammy, don't be so melodramatic. Nobody cares about reputations any longer.'

'Well, *I* do.' She banged her fist down on the table. 'And anyway, you know what Luscombe's like. It's in a time warp—and you know very well what everybody will think.'

'Nonsense. Why on earth should they?'

'As I said—you here, and me like this.' She gestured angrily at herself.

Zak roared with laughter as his glance skimmed over the ample undulations of candlewick. 'For heaven's sake, the whole idea's ludicrous!'

'Oh?' Stung by his casual hilarity, she glowered at him. 'And just why is it so ludicrous?'

He caught her eye, and reluctantly straightened his face, then shrugged. 'Well, you know, you're just a——' He stopped, then went on, 'We've known each other all our lives—you're like my kid sister.'

Tamsin stared at him, all her heated words freezing in her throat. Of course, he was right. It was only her wholly new, heightened awareness of him—and her urgent anxiety to keep it from him— that had made her react so violently. A thin little kid, in a too-large schoolgirl dressing-gown. That was how Zak—and every postman in Devon—saw her. She'd been a fool to imagine anything else.

And in any case, it was surely much better, much safer that way. She was feeling more than enough shame and embarrassment now—just how would it be if he were ever to discover the truth? That, far from being the child he still comfortably saw her as, she was a grown woman, and with the sexual desires of a grown woman.

Zak must have glimpsed at least something of this in her face, for he swore, then, coming across to her, put his arm round her shoulders, pulling her to him.

'Oh, Tam, why do you always bring out the worst in me? Look, we've both had a long night. Sit down and have some breakfast.'

He hooked a chair away from the table, gave her a gentle shove down on to it, then turned back to the stove. Tamsin sat, her head resting in her cupped hand, letting the warmth of the kitchen envelop her like an eiderdown. Dimly she could hear the clink of china, smell the fragrance of freshly brewed coffee, see the dark outline that was Zak moving around.

Gradually, though, as her head slid from her hand down her arm, to rest in the crook of her elbow, even that outline lost substance until it became a vague shadow. The shadow was standing over her now, talking to her, lifting her head, but the fatigue had taken command of her body. She felt a pair of strong arms go round her and mumbled in protest, but as they lifted her clean out of the chair she surrendered, tumbling down into black oblivion...

A blackbird was stridently proclaiming his territory in the old pear tree on the wall outside her bedroom window; yellow sunlight was pouring in through the chintz curtains. Tamsin rolled over, then, as she remembered, she lay still, staring at the ceiling beam just above her head.

Zak...Jack Beasley...her foolish reaction... then those hands lifting her effortlessly. Just for a moment she allowed herself the pleasure of remembering, through the haze of sleep, the feel of those strong arms about her. What would it be like, to be held in a loving embrace by those arms, she thought drowsily—held all night long, and to be awakened into love by his slow, seductive kisses?

But then she forced the treacherous images from her mind and, pushing back the bedclothes, sat up. Glancing at the bedside clock, she saw with astonishment that it was midday. But the alarm had been switched off; Zak must have done that, as well as fetching her the hot-water bottle that was now cold at her feet. What a contradiction he was. Tough, uncompromising, hard through and through, and yet, as she'd seen last night, like all thoroughly masculine men, capable of a feminine sensitivity which could bring tears to the eyes.

As she rolled out of bed, blinking away those tears, she realised with a wash of relief that she was still wearing her dressing-gown. At least he hadn't undressed her. Although even if he had—her mouth gave a bitter little twist—he would no doubt only have viewed her as just another pathetic little scrap of a lamb.

And for her part, she mustn't allow herself to see him as anything other than her enemy. After last night she could so easily have been lulled into dropping her guard, but she knew Zak too well even to allow herself to hope that anything had changed as far as his designs on Wethertor were concerned.

As for her feelings for him—well, she could admit them, take them out into the daylight and look at them for what they were, but then she must thrust

them back into the darkness where they belonged.
To do anything else—to allow them to grow into
anything else—would be fatal for herself, just as it
had been for Sarah, who had loved Zak and been
destroyed by that love.

'Oh, *no!*'

Tamsin jabbed one final time at the lever, then
climbed down from the tractor seat. The hoist
mechanism on the trailer had gone yet again, which
meant, yet again, a repair bill from Jim Hewitt's
garage—or even worse, that this time Jim would
not be able to work any more of his magic. After
all, these days you could see veteran vehicles in
better shape than this one lovingly polished and restored in any bygone farming museum.

Ah well, there was nothing for it. She'd have to
load up the trailer by hand—and soon, before
Matthew came back from checking the stock, and
tried to insist on doing the job for her. Aiming a
vicious kick at the nearest tyre, Tamsin snatched
up the pitchfork and, wrinkling up her nose in distaste, clambered up on to the gently steaming
mound of well-rotted farmyard manure.

She had been working for half an hour or so,
establishing an easy rhythm, when out of the very
corner of her eye she saw two riders on the old
bridleway to the moor, which passed right alongside
her yard wall. They were still quite a distance away,
but one of them sat astride his black horse with an
upright, easy grace that was quite unmistakable.

Glancing down at her dungarees, wellington boots and out-at-the-elbows navy sweater, she stifled an anguished moan, but somehow resisted the impulse to fling down her pitchfork and take refuge in the barn. Instead she tightened her grip on it and went on methodically with her task.

In and out went the metal prongs, and no load of manure was ever placed more delicately in a battered old trailer. The granite wall was high over here in the corner of the yard; if she worked quietly enough, they could very well pass without even realising she was there.

'Morning, Tamsin.'

Reluctantly, she looked up and found herself eyeball to eyeball with Zak. He was leaning sideways in the saddle, one arm negligently resting along the top of the wall, and surveying her in such a way that she felt exactly as she'd done when, at the age of five, she'd been discovered playing sandcastles with a pile of rich velvety soot, left behind by the sweep for her mother's rose bed.

'Morning,' she muttered.

After a quick half-glance, her eyes skittered away to his companion and she hastily tacked a slightly more gracious expression on to her features, even as she groaned inwardly.

The woman was a newcomer to the village; Tamsin had only seen her a couple of times in the distance, once coming out of the post office, once in Church Lane getting into a low-slung sports car outside the Victorian red brick house she had bought. Both times, she had been immaculately dressed in outfits which, even to Tamsin's normally uninterested eyes, had spelt 'Designer', and for fully ten minutes afterwards she had ached with insubstantial longings.

This morning the woman had on faultless cream gabardine breeches and plum-coloured jacket, while under the hard hat every strand of blonde hair was in its place. Zak, too, was impeccably turned out, in breeches, tailored black jacket, and white shirt. In the old days, no one would ever have got him into an outfit like this; with his anarchic attitude to everything respectable, he regarded formal riding gear as affectation, and took a wicked delight in giving the ageing Master of Foxhounds apoplexy by turning up for the hunt in old jeans and threadbare polo sweater, while from under the rim of his disreputable riding hat, which was jammed down over his unruly black hair, grey eyes would gleam with mischief.

And yet here he was, looking like any other correct, upper-class Englishman. As she stared at him, a tight hand squeezing painfully on her ribs, Tamsin felt the hectic colour which had risen in her cheeks fade, until she was rather paler than before.

She realised that Zak was speaking. 'Have you met Yolande?'

'I—no.' Tamsin managed a polite nod at the woman, who gave her a warm smile in return.

'Hello, Tamsin.'

Leaning down from her horse, she stretched out her hand and Tamsin, after a moment's surprise,

polished a grubby paw against her dungarees and
shook hands.

'Zak's offered to show me the moor,' Yolande
went on. She pulled a face. 'Do you know, I've
been here nearly three months now, and I've still
seen hardly anything of it?'

'Really?' Tamsin replied politely. 'Well, it always
takes time to settle in.'

'We're going to a waterfall that Zak's been telling
me about—right off the beaten track——'

'Our valley,' Zak cut in. 'Do you remember,
Tam—that place we used to ride to when we were
kids?'

She closed her eyes momentarily against the pain
that ripped through her. Could he really imagine
for one moment that she would ever forget that
hidden, magical place? They'd even called it the
Secret Valley, and kept it a cherished secret for just
the three of them. And now here he was, betraying
it to this outsider.

'Yes, I remember,' she said woodenly.

'Fancy coming with us?'

She stared at him. He knew she couldn't possibly—the offer was as casual, and as empty, as those
he had tossed out to her years before, even after
Sarah had hinted that he didn't want her tagging
along with them so often. After that, pride, that
stiff little backbone of hers, had prevented her from
intruding ever again, and she'd always replied, just
as she did now, 'Oh, no, thanks. I'm far too busy.'

'Well, lambing's over, surely?'

'Yes, we finished a week ago.'

'And how are they?'

'Going on well.'

She wanted to thank him again for his help, but somehow she could not bring herself to mention that night. She was horribly aware of Yolande's eyes on her, and knew that even the most oblique mention of it would be enough to bring the betraying colour to her cheeks.

'Well, if you're sure.' He straightened up. 'Ready, Yolande?'

The young woman nodded, and with a casual salute of his riding crop he led the way, clattering off up the track. Tamsin stood, watching, and felt the bitter gall of jealousy churn inside her.

When they were at last out of sight, she went to begin work again, but then, as she moved, she heard a loud squelch, and looking down saw that her boots were gently subsiding into the manure. Another time she might have laughed, but today, her face set, she grimly thrust the pitchfork in to steady herself and heaved out first one foot, then the other.

She was clambering down from the heap, when Matthew came across the yard to her.

'Now you should have let me do that, Tamsin.'

'I've managed it, thanks, Matthew.'

'Was that Mrs Chalmers I saw with Master Zachary? Very pleasant young woman, she is.'

'Yes.' Tamsin's back was to him.

'So they've gone out riding, have they? They've been seen about together a fair bit lately.' He paused significantly. 'Folk say in the village she's getting over a nasty divorce, so perhaps they two——'

'How are the lambs?' The words were jerked out of her.

'Oh, fine, nothing to worry about there. Yes— a beautifully turned out young lady she is, always. I do like to see a smartly dressed woman.'

And Tamsin could only give a pallid smile of agreement, and thrust the pitchfork into the heap, as though she were plunging it into Dracula's vitals.

CHAPTER SIX

THE long curving flight of steps was before Tamsin, and picking up the wide skirts of her pink ballgown, she drifted down them. Waiting in the shadows below was a man in evening dress. He walked out into the light, and it was Zak. As he watched her, his expression was dazed, like that of a sleep-walker who has been roughly woken.

'My darling Tammy,' he breathed, 'how beautiful you are.' And leaning forward, he gently touched her lips with the tips of his fingers. As his eyes locked with hers, she saw them darken to a stormy grey, and he pulled her violently to him. He dragged at the tie-belt of her dress and it parted to reveal that beneath it she was naked——

Fiercely, Tamsin shook herself free of the daydream and took a vicious bite out of the sandwich which had hung suspended in her hand for at least five minutes. That's all I need, she thought despairingly, to start weaving sexual fantasies around Zak. She seemed to have spent most of the last few nights dreaming about him, and now here he was elbowing his way into her days as well.

But, of course, fantasies were always an escape from real life, weren't they? And she certainly had plenty to escape from just now, she thought ruefully. Bills, always bills—hurtling at her as though off a never-ending conveyor belt: her feed supplier, who had always until now been so understanding, pressing for payment, and this morning's latest epistle from the bank manager 'inviting' her in for a little chat about her situation, at her earliest convenience.

And then there was Matthew, and the shame of knowing that, for all his hard work, she was paying him no more than pocket money. She'd really needed him yesterday, though, when the butcher's truck had arrived for the pigs, and he'd taken over when she'd . . .

Tamsin stared into the middle distance, her eyes shadowed. Was it possible that, after spending her whole life on a farm, she wasn't really cut out to be a farmer after all? She sighed, sensed that vertical frown line between her brows slip into place again—not that it ever seemed to be absent for long these days—and felt the almost physical pressure, as though a heavy weight were pressing down on her slim shoulders.

With another faint sigh, she crammed in the last of her sandwich, screwed the top back on her vacuum flask and climbed on to the tractor again. As she reached forward to switch on the ignition, though, she paused. There, surely, was that same hot-air balloon which she'd seen the previous morning. It was floating down the valley towards her, like a huge orange and white bubble, quite soundless, until, as she screwed up her eyes to peer at it, she heard a faint sibilant hiss.

As she watched, captivated, it lifted gently higher into the air and drifted away, over the rocky slopes of Wether Tor. How beautiful it was, that fragile bubble, and how wonderful it must be to ride in it, with its giant's eye view of the earth far below. Way above such things as unpaid bills and bank managers' letters, that cold, sneaky voice put in.

All at once, she thought, Oh, God, is it all worth it? Then, with a lurch of sick fear, Am I going to make it in the end, or am I just running faster and faster into a blind alley? Whatever the answer, she had work to do, so, ramming the tractor into gear, she began spreading the fertiliser again.

It was only when a dark shadow brushed across her face that she looked up, startled. The balloon was directly overhead, barely more than fifty feet up, so that she could see the two figures in the basket slung beneath it. As she watched, it crossed the field, lurched down on a patch of level ground on the far side of the stream, bounced gently, then touched earth again.

One of the figures clambered out rather awkwardly and caught hold of the basket, then a voice shouted something that sounded like, 'Come here!'

She sat where she was, though, staring, until the man glanced round, and this time she heard the impatient 'Tammy, come here, will you?' clearly enough, so she scrambled down from the tractor and began running towards them.

'Here—catch hold.' Zak was almost out of breath with the effort of struggling single-handed to tether the flying creature to the ground.

She seized the other side of the leather-bound rim, gritting her teeth as her arms almost wrenched out of their sockets; the great bubble swayed overhead one final time, then sagged softly down on to the grass.

A Jeep came bucketing across the open moor and three men jumped out, caught firm hold of the basket, then dexterously secured the retaining ropes. Loosing her grip, Tamsin gingerly flexed her shoulders and dared to look directly at Zak for the first time. He was laughing with exhilaration, his grey eyes sparkling, and at the sight of him, looking as he'd so often done after some daredevil prank, she felt that tight band of heaviness instantly knot itself into place round her stomach again.

'Thanks, Tam.'

He unzipped his scarlet quilted parka and grinned down at her, his teeth white against his tanned features. But she could not return the smile. Her whole body seemed to throb with a barely controllable longing to touch him, to hold him to her, but she couldn't do that, so instead she said rather coldly, 'I hope you haven't frightened my sheep.'

'Now would I?'

He shook his head good-humouredly, then turned to help the others. Tamsin backed away from the group and stood, her hands jammed into her anorak pockets, listening to a lively conversation about burners, lines, the envelope, and always, with every particle of her being, aware of Zak. But he had forgotten all about her—they all had, in this man's world—so finally she turned away, her shoulders drooping slightly.

'Hey, Tam, come for a ride.'

It was more of a royal command than an invitation, but she backed away as he advanced on her.

'No, thank you.'

'Oh, come on, it's great up there.'

'No, I'd really rather not,' she said stiffly. She was finding that she couldn't look at him, so instead she spoke to his fourth shirt button.

'What's the matter? Not frightened, surely?' He dropped his voice. 'I dare you.'

The sneaky swine! He knew she'd never refused a dare in her life. On the other hand, if she fell out of the basket, she'd have more than the concussion and dislocated shoulder she'd got when he'd dared her to walk across the stable roof.

'Come on,' he urged.

When she risked a quick glance, he was smiling down at her, that wholly irresistible smile of his. Beyond him, the other man was doing something complicated with the burners and she thought, At least I shan't be up there alone with Zak, which would be quite unbearable, and heard herself saying weakly, 'Well, perhaps——'

Next moment he had caught her round the waist and was swinging her over into the wicker basket. She gave the man a pale smile and he winked at her encouragingly, then, as Zak lifted a long leg over the edge and hauled himself in, he leapt nimbly out to join the rest of the team on the ground.

'I-isn't he coming?'

'No, not this time.'

He shot her a challenging look, and because she couldn't let him think her a coward she stayed where she was, clutching the rim with hands that had suddenly become clammy and staring fixedly at the rocks which crowned the distant summit of Wether Tor.

All too swiftly, the balloon was reinflated from a portable gas cylinder, the ropes were loosening and above their heads the orange and white fabric swayed as it met the wind and bounded skywards.

'Are you going to keep your eyes closed all the time?' Zak's voice was at her ear.

'Of course I'm not!' she retorted indignantly, and cautiously opened first one eye, and then, with a long, breathy 'Oh-h-h!' the other.

Already far below them were the tiny squares of field and pasture, broken here and there by patches of woodland. There in the valley was Luscombe village, with its grey stone church, the Manor House—Zak's home—completely surrounded by an ocean of pink and mauve rhododendron bushes, and the thatched roofs and white cob walls of the cottages, looking exactly like a child's toy. Beyond was the great granite expanse of the moor, rolling away to the horizon where, very faintly, she could see the glittering line of the sea.

'Oh, it's marvellous!' She shook her head in wonderment.

'Yes, it is, isn't it? I really think I'll take some ballooning lessons.'

She jerked round to him, her eyes widening with terror. 'You mean you haven't had any?'

'Of course I have.' Zak gave her a disarming grin. 'Don't worry, Tam. I was only teasing.'

'Oh.'

But as she relaxed, he went on casually, 'Yes, I had one yesterday—and a dozen before that,' he added, as he caught her eye and relented. 'You surely don't imagine I'd risk bringing you up here if I didn't know what I was doing, do you?'

'I don't know.' She grimaced. 'After all, you're always telling me I'm in your way, so it would be a perfect chance to get rid of me.'

'True, I hadn't thought of that. Maybe you'd better not stand too near the edge—it might be too tempting for me. Anyway, you like my new toy, do you?'

'It's yours, then, is it?' She tried not to sound too impressed.

'Of course—or at least, Trenchard Enterprises'. It's the latest addition to our range of executive goodies. When they get tired of knocking hell out of clay pigeons—or flogging Jags round the circuit—we'll bring them up here for a couple of hours, then send them home, tired but happy, and a couple of hundred quid lighter.'

He peered down at the ground. 'Look, there's Luscombe Man down there.'

'Where? I can't see it.'

'There.' He gestured with one hand, then without warning put an arm round her shoulders, and, before she could even tense, pulled her across to stand in front of him. 'Follow the skyline down to that patch of gorse, then——'

'Oh, yes, I see it,' as she finally located the little matchstick which was Luscombe Man, the massive granite stone, three times the height of a man, which had stood alone on the moor for the last five thousand years. She shivered, as a bat's wing of the same superstitious terror that she'd felt as a child for this towering stone brushed across her mind.

'It'll soon be May Day again,' said Zak. 'That's one thing I've missed the last few years. Will you be going to the Ritual?'

'I-I expect so,' she replied, but she had barely heard the question. Zak was resting his chin on the top of her head; his breath was stirring the fine tendrils at her hairline, while, folded in his arms, she could feel the hard length of his body. Just for a moment, she let herself relax into him, leaning against him, as a secret, forbidden thrill ran through her. He smelled wonderful: of fresh air, heather and gorse, and the warm, vibrant maleness of him was all around her——

'We're losing height.'

Abruptly, he loosed her and turned to the burner, releasing a gush of flame that roared upwards, and a moment later she felt, beneath her feet, the basket sway softly, then lift. His eyes were gleaming silver-grey with exuberance, and the wind was ruffling his black hair, so that a lock fell across his brow. He looked across at her and grinned. 'All right?'

'Yes.'

'But she wasn't. For in that split second she had realised, finally, the truth. When had it happened? she wondered dully. At what precise moment had her feelings for Zak leapt unnoticed across that great divide? Or maybe it was that love had always been there, disguised as a child's hero-worship, a teenager's crush—or even a woman's sexual longings. Whatever the reality, she would never be able to blind herself to the truth again. She loved him. She said the words silently inside herself. But the knowledge brought her no joy, only a strange, despairing kind of calm.

'Are you sure you're all right?' He tilted her chin, looking at her closely. 'You're very pale. We can go down as soon as you like.'

'No—no, I'm fine.' But her lips were so stiff that she could hardly form the words.

She moved her head back from the warm touch of his fingers and looked down, veiling her eyes with her lashes, terrified of what his penetrating gaze might read there. One part of her wanted desperately to be back on the ground, away from this dangerous, betraying intimacy; the other yearned to stay up here with Zak forever, in this magical, floating, utterly secret world.

Together they stood, his arm lightly brushing hers, looking down. They had drifted away from the village now and were over the open moor.

'All the time I was away I dreamed of this place, you know,' he said softly. 'There's no place like it on earth, is there?'

'No, there isn't,' she replied tremulously. Even something as innocuous as their shared love for the moor could, she was rapidly discovering, cause her intense anguish.

'Mind you, in a few weeks' time, I'll be flying over a slightly different terrain,' Zak added.

'Oh?'

'Yes, I'll be ballooning across the Grand Canyon.'

'What, in the States, you mean?'

'That's right. An ex-Army pal of mine runs some of those adventure-type holidays, and I'm thinking of incorporating them in my packages—the ultimate dream, and all that.'

'You'll be going away soon, then?' A wild half-hope, half-desolation was flaring in her.

'Yes.' He eyed her sardonically. 'But don't worry. I'll be back within the week.'

'Oh.' Her nail was picking busily at a rough snag in the leather edging of the basket. 'So you really are here to stay this time?'

'Of course,' he said coolly. 'I've already told you, haven't I?'

'Yes, but——'

'Why shouldn't I?'

'I don't know. I suppose it's just that most of your—enthusiasms have always been pretty short-lived.'

'Sorry to disappoint you,' he was more than matching the slight edge in her voice, 'but I haven't changed my mind. I'm here to stay from now on. And in case you're wondering, yes, I've made it up with my father. Not that we shall ever be the best of friends, exactly,' for a moment, the old bitterness was there, 'but we've achieved what I suppose you could describe as an unarmed truce.'

'H-how is he?' In spite of herself, Tamsin felt the stirrings of pity for the once-active man, now a bedridden invalid.

'As well as can be expected—that's the usual phrase, isn't it?'

'I'm sorry, Zak.' She heard herself say the words she'd never thought she would say and, even more horrified, saw herself slip her small hand into his large tanned one.

He held it, looking down at it as it lay in his, his thumb stroking across a callus on her palm. 'Well, I'm doing all I can. He's in an excellent nursing home in Torbay—twenty-four-hour nursing and all that—and I get down there as often as possible. I was there last night, as a matter of fact.' He paused. 'We were talking about you.'

'Oh?'

His fingers closed on hers before she could withdraw her hand.

'Yes, it seems as if you were right. I don't know whether his conscience has been pricking him or what, but he admits now that your father was put under—some pressure to buy Wethertor.'

'Well, that's generous of him.'

Tamsin could not restrain the bitter retort, but he gently put a finger on her lips to silence her and went on, 'So I—that is, we have decided that it would be fair to increase our offer.'

'What do you mean?'

'We'll give you what your father gave for the land four years ago—and that's a price way above its present-day value.'

This time she snatched her hand away. 'No.'

'Why the hell not?' His black brows came down in a furious scowl.

'Because I'm not in the market for charity, that's why.'

She knew that in a saner, cooler moment, she was going to regret this impetuous act of madness, but her pride simply would not allow her to stand, begging bowl in hand, ready to touch her forelock in grateful submission to a Trenchard—and particularly this one.

Zak banged his fists down on the side of the basket. 'It's that damned Westmacott pride again.'

She almost leapt clean through her skin at his uncanny picking up of her thought-waves, then hastily translated her nervous start into jamming her hands hard into her anorak pockets.

'If you like—yes. But in any case, nothing's changed.' She forced from her mind her own earlier doubts and fears, when for all of five minutes she had allowed herself to contemplate defeat. 'Wethertor is not for sale.'

Zak took a furious step towards her and for one terrifying second she really wondered if he was going to snatch her up and throw her over the side. Instead, though, he reached for her and roughly pulled her into his arms, his fingers biting cruelly into her flesh. His face came down towards her, blotting out the sunlight, then, as she gave a half-fearful gasp, his mouth closed on hers, his lips scorching her. The heat from his mouth was spreading to her entire body, melting her muscles, her bones, burning her up from the inside.

But then she sensed, almost imperceptibly, Zak's fury fading. The angry kiss was becoming something else—something that was even more intimidating. His hands fractionally released their grasp and his lips began to trail fluttering butterfly wings across her scarlet cheek.

'Tammy.' His voice was a sensuous murmur in her ear.

Just five minutes ago, she'd realised that she loved him. Now she was in his arms, being caressed, kissed by him. She closed her eyes and clung to him, surrendering herself entirely to his possession.

Surrendering! Herself—her land! Her eyes flew open, and with her last strength she tore herself free from him, pressing herself against the very edge of the swaying basket.

'I s-suppose——' her teeth were chattering so that she could scarcely get the words out '—I suppose that's the Trenchard version of friendly persuasion?'

'What the hell do you mean?' He was breathing deeply, and there was an angry flush on his cheekbones.

'Oh—turn on a bit of the heavy stuff, and I give in.'

'For God's sake!' He gave a sneering laugh. 'I just might try that sort of thing if you were a real woman, but—well, I'd be wasting my time with a child like you, wouldn't I?'

And, thrusting his hands into his pockets, he turned his back on her and stood staring out over the moor.

For long moments, Tamsin gazed at that back. The wind was getting up, making her eyes sting; if he turned round again now, he'd think she was crying. The warmth of his arms, his lips, was on her still and she longed to take the single stride to him, put her arms around him, lay her cheek against his shoulder and say softly, 'You're wrong, Zak. I'm not a child any more—I *am* a real woman.'

But instead, setting her lips into a tight line, she too turned away. This was why he'd brought her up here, of course. Not for the pleasure of her company, as she'd foolishly half allowed herself to hope, but simply as the next round in his campaign. Trap her in this confined space, where there was nowhere for her to run, and then start turning the screws once more...

'Look, Tammy.' She realised that he had turned and was within hands' touching distance of her again. 'I know how much Wethertor—the house, I mean—matters to you. It must hold a lot of memories for you, and I really don't want to force you out of it.'

She eyed him warily. He sounded perfectly sincere, but—just what was he up to now?

'So how about if you go on living there, in part of it at least? We could turn some of the upstairs into a self-contained flat. You could stay there—and work for me.'

'Doing what, precisely?'

'Well, all my paperwork is getting into a hell of a mess.' He grinned ruefully. 'What I need is a Girl Friday to keep me in order. You could have an office in the Manor and——'

'B-but I don't know anything about office work!' Stunned by the suddenness of his offer, Tamsin was having problems thinking coherently.

'I seem to remember you did typing and book-keeping at school.'

'No!' She shook her head vehemently.

'You're bound to be a bit rusty at first, but you're pretty bright—you'll soon pick it up.'

'No. I don't want to work in an office.' But it wasn't that—it was the thought of seeing Zak every day, of working in such close proximity with him, that put the violence into her tone. 'I'm a farmer and——'

'Hello. What's happened to all those pigs of yours?'

'What?'

As she stared at him, bewildered by his apparent change of tack, he gestured downwards and she realised that the veering wind had brought them back over the farm.

'They've gone,' she said shortly.

'Oh?' He reached out and tilted her face so that she was forced to meet his eyes. 'I suppose they're the first you've had to send off for slaughter, are they?'

'Yes.'

He looked down at her, a little smile playing around his mouth. 'I remember how you always used to hide yourself away in the cupboard under the stairs. But you can't hide now, can you?'

When she did not reply, he went on remorselessly, 'And what will you do when those lambs get big enough to send to market—that little black one, for instance?'

'Shut up, damn you!' she said through her teeth.

He shook his head sadly at her. 'You'll never make a farmer, Tam. You know that, don't you?'

But what else *can* I do? The words were almost blurted out, but she bit them back.

All at once he swivelled her round from him and jabbed a finger down towards the ground. 'Look there. You may refuse to see it from ground level, but from up here it's so obvious. There's your land—the wood and the tor running straight as an arrow into mine. Even you must see that we can't operate so successfully with that lot,' another angry jab of the finger, 'damn near slicing us in two.'

She stood motionless, staring down almost unseeingly at the back-up vehicle, which, far below, was lurching over the rough terrain in dogged pursuit of them. Zak was utterly implacable; he would go on and on and on—water wearing away a rock—until he got what he wanted, because that was Zak Trenchard—a man who never thought of giving up, until by one means or another he got his own way. Horrified, she thought she could actually feel the physical sensation of her will-power melting in the fire of his determination.

Her shoulders sagged wearily. What was the point in fighting him any longer? And besides, he was going to be here for the rest of her life, and how could she bear that? She wouldn't work for him—that, at least, she was certain of—but even so she would see him almost every day, sometimes unexpectedly, so that she had no time to arm herself with cool indifference.

Maybe he'd marry—Yolande, perhaps—have children. And with that acute, all-seeing eye of his, wouldn't he, sooner or later, come to realise her feelings for him? Maybe they'd even joke about her. Little Tammy? Oh, yes, she's carried a torch for me since the age of four... Long years of endless night.

Of course, she might in time get over him, just as the first sharp pain of losing her father and Sarah had dulled. Sarah. Her lips twisted. What a bitter irony, that the man who'd destroyed one friend's chance of happiness was now——

Her only hope was to get away *now*, before it was too late. Maybe if she never saw him again, she might recover from this sickness in her blood. Yes, that was the answer; she knew it, with ice-cold clarity.

'You know it makes sense, don't you?' Zak was speaking, more softly now. He must have sensed her weakening, and was moving in for the kill.

'Makes sense?' she said bleakly. 'Well, perhaps.'

Instantly he had snatched her up into his arms, both feet dangling, so that the basket swayed, and kissed her cheek. 'You won't regret it, Tammy. I know you won't.'

She flinched away out of his arms, the tingling warmth of his lips threatening to break through the chilling numbness that was taking hold of her.

'I'll give my solicitor a ring as soon as I get back—I'm seeing him tomorrow, anyway.'

'No!' The panic flared in her. She mustn't let him push her this fast, not when she was so vulnerable. 'Give me a few days to think about it, please, Zak—a week,' she pleaded.

He frowned slightly. 'I'll give you three days— or it'll be valued on current prices.'

'All right, three days.' Her mouth was so full of the dry ashes of despair that she could scarcely get the words out. 'Now, please take me down.'

He reached up and pulled hard on the rip-cord, so that they began to descend.

'You'll have to come up again some time soon.' In his barely suppressed triumph, he was all affability. 'You enjoyed it once we were up there, didn't you?'

Tamsin nodded, even managed some sort of smile, but she was too full up with emotion to speak.

Zak let his arm rest casually on her shoulder for a moment. 'You always were a great little sport, Tam.'

The balloon landed with a bump and she scrambled out. That was how she'd go down in history, she thought as she grimly hung on to one of the ropes. Tamsin Westmacott, the great little sport.

CHAPTER SEVEN

'But I can't possibly accept it, Liz.' Tamsin turned back from the mirror to her friend, sitting cross-legged on the bed.

'Nonsense—of course you can. I've told you, after the twins, I shall never get into a size ten anything ever again.' Liz patted her ample hips. 'It was always a struggle—and anyway, Rob says I'm better with a bit more meat on my bones.' And at her loving tone, Tamsin could not wholly quell the small, involuntary sting of pain.

'In any case,' Liz went on, 'it was never really right for me, and it suits you perfectly. Here, put the jacket on.'

She tossed it at Tamsin, who obediently slipped it on, then stood back, gazing spellbound at her reflection.

It was incredible. Her old brown skirt and sweater lay in a heap on the chair, just like a chrysalis from which—a chic butterfly had just emerged. Under the collarless black jersey jacket the long-sleeved polyester satin blouse fitted her like a second skin, the hand-pin-tucked front moulding to the outline of her small, high breasts, now cradled in one of Liz's dainty little cast-off bras, a half-cup in beige lace-edged silk.

And the shocking pink of the blouse set off her light tan beautifully, giving a sheen to her skin and a sparkle to her green eyes. She half turned, in an unconscious preen, and the straight black jersey skirt clung seductively to her slender hips as she moved.

'You look great, love, you really do.'

Tamsin flushed, then smiled. 'It's beautiful, Liz—but it was so expensive. I really can't take it.'

'Look, I'm honestly not doing you any great favour. It's last year's fashion.' Tamsin suppressed a little smile; was this the Liz Ayres who, only yesterday—or so it seemed—had been never happier than in jeans and an ancient sweat-shirt? 'So don't go getting on that high horse of yours. If you don't have it, I shall only give it to Ingeborg, and she's had quite enough of my stuff already.'

'Well——'

'Of course, it's a bit short. If you take it off, I'll get——'

'No!' Tamsin heard herself exclaim violently. Possessively, she smoothed down the soft, luxurious jersey across her flat stomach, then, catching her friend's eye, grinned shamefacedly. 'Thanks, Liz.'

'My pleasure. And yes, I *should* keep it on.' Liz gave Tamsin a teasing smile. 'I'm taking you out to lunch—after our session in the salon.'

'Oh, but——'

'No buts. Rob can stand it. Or rather,' Liz winked wickedly, 'his credit card can. I don't lure you down here half often enough, so we're really going to hit the town. Now, you finish getting ready, while I have a word with Inge.'

Tamsin smiled, rather tremulously, but did not argue any more. Liz was obviously determined to spoil her, and, if she was honest, a bit of spoiling, just now, was something she could happily put up with.

She stood listening, first to the footsteps clattering down the stairs, then to the high-pitched, exuberant conversation in the kitchen below. Dear Liz! At twenty-two, less than a year older than she was and, after Sarah, her best friend from schooldays, here she was, already in possession of an adoring husband, who ran his own factory in a new industrial development on the outskirts of town, a lovely house, a Swedish au pair, and the utterly enchanting six-month-old Adam and Mark.

Just for a moment, Tamsin felt a stab of wholly uncharacteristic envy as she thought of her own lifestyle, but then thrust it away from her. *Her* life was about to change—and for the better. Exactly how, she still wasn't sure—in fact, that was why she had rung Liz to take up the long-standing invitation to visit her in Plymouth.

The previous afternoon, after that traumatic ride through the sky, she had somehow driven the tractor back to the farm and shut herself away in the house, away from Matthew, away even from Joss. She'd paced up and down the chilly, never-used parlour and there, among the white-dust-sheeted furniture, she had tried, grim-eyed, to confront her future.

The one thing she'd been clear about was that her instant, horrified rejection of Zak's offer of a job had been right. She either had to remain as she was—or make a clean, brutal break. But here, in the beloved house itself, with all the memories it held for her, it had been impossible to come to any conclusion, and so, feeling as though she would suffocate if she stayed in the room a moment longer, she'd almost run to the kitchen to ring Liz.

'And two green salads, please.'

As Liz handed the menu cards back to the waiter, Tamsin looked around her at the restaurant décor, which managed to be luxurious yet at the same time pretty, with its dainty bamboo trellis-work and pine tables in alcoves of greenery. Leaning across, she rubbed a green and white coleus leaf between her fingers.

'Good grief, it's plastic!'

Liz pulled a face. 'Oh, dear. Still, they look almost better than the real thing, don't they—and no dead leaves?' She took a bite of her bread roll. 'I hope they hurry up—I'm ravenous! Derek certainly took his time with your hair.'

Tamsin rolled her eyes. 'Yes. I got the distinct impression that he'd never had to deal with hair like it before, and hoped he never would again. I thought he was never going to stop lecturing me about regular cutting, conditioning——'

'But it was worth it.' Liz studied the finished product complacently. 'You look absolutely stunning! Those blonde highlights really set off your face, and that upswept style—it's *great*.'

Tamsin gingerly put a neat pink pearl fingertip to the gleaming pile of hair that had been blow-dried and hot-combed into a mass of feathery blonde-streaked curls on top of her head.

'And that make-up—it really suits you, the way it brings out the colour of your eyes. You should wear it all the time, you know.'

'But I'd frighten the sheep out of their wits,' Tamsin protested half-heartedly.

'Yes, well, you won't have to worry about their opinion much longer, will you? *Will* you?' Liz repeated meaningfully.

For a moment Tamsin hesitated, then, 'No, you're right.'

And as she said it, she felt herself relax, as the enormous burden she'd carried for so long seemed to lift from her slender shoulders a fraction. She hadn't told Liz the whole truth—somehow she had recoiled from the inevitable pity that she would see in her friend's eyes at the recounting of the pathetic little story of her love for Zak—but Liz had been quite clear about what Tamsin should do.

And she was right, of course. Away from Wethertor she could, as she'd hoped, see that. The farm *was* too much for her—the only sensible thing was to give it up. But that's not why you're leaving, is it? that sneaky little voice whispered. You're leaving because of Zak Trenchard. OK, but what if I am? Does it matter? Not in the slightest, she told herself fiercely, then roused to hear Liz say,

'We must drink to your new life, Tamsin. Let's have champagne. I can just see you in that gorgeous apartment on the Hoe——' the flat she'd insisted on taking Tamsin to inspect on their way to the salon. 'There's a wonderful view of the sea—— '

Yes, and if I stand on tiptoe at the bathroom window, I can even see one tiny corner of the moor. But Tamsin put the intrusive thought from her. Liz was so pleased and happy, in an almost childlike way, to be planning her life for her, that she might as well relax and enjoy it.

'To the new Tamsin Westmacott. May she find fame and fortune,' Liz intoned solemnly, then they clinked glasses, giggling as the icy bubbles slid down their throats.

They were not the only ones celebrating. Another bottle of champagne, cradled in its ice-bed, was making its stately way through the crowded restaurant to the couple in the next alcove but one. Tamsin edged forward slightly, then all at once went very still. Abruptly she set down her glass, so that a little of the liquid spilled in tiny bubbles across the back of her hand.

They were facing one another, so that she only saw them in profile. Yolande was wearing a flower-splashed dress in some silky material, Zak a dark grey suit and white shirt. His black hair, for once, was subdued into neatness; he leaned across to say something, smile at the woman with him, then went back to studying the menu, that little frown of concentration, which she knew so well, creasing his brow.

Barely half aware of Liz chattering on, Tamsin was staring at him when, without warning, almost as though the touch of her gaze had brushed like fingers across his face, he turned abruptly. Before she could duck behind the potted greenery his gaze fell on her, paused for an instant, but then, even as their glances met, he looked past her—no, right through her, she amended, uncertain whether to be angry or weak with relief—then turned all his attention back to Yolande.

Was he ignoring her? No, there had not been the slightest hint of recognition in his casual glance. Either he was totally preoccupied with his companion or, even worse, in her new feminine guise she was totally unrecognisable. He probably wouldn't even notice her if she were to leap up on to their table, kick the ice bucket out of the way, and perform a slow erotic strip-tease. Or if he did, he'd only smile that maddeningly indulgent smile of his, tell her not to be a silly little girl, and to put her clothes back on straight away...

The delicious meal went down untasted. Tamsin dutifully chewed and swallowed, but she could as well have been eating the contents of one of the kitchen rubbish bins, and when Liz said, 'Don't you think that's a great idea, Tamsin?' she nodded fervently, then discovered that she had agreed to Rob talking to his contacts in town about finding her a job, temporary at first perhaps, until she had time to look around.

The other two were obviously in high spirits, and Tamsin, every fibre of her being strained towards that table, those two heads so close together, sensed that the jubilation was absolutely nothing at all to do with the champagne. But she could make out nothing of what they were saying until, as Zak raised his glass for a toast, all of a sudden one of those strange little silences which happened sometimes in the most crowded of rooms, when everyone simultaneously fell quiet, occurred and she heard his deep voice, carrying clearly across to her: 'To Trenchard Enterprises—our continued success, and confusion to the rest.'

'Are you all right, Tamsin?'

From very far away, she emerged to meet Liz's anxious eyes.

'I——' she began, then stopped.

'Is it too warm in here for you? I'll get someone to open a window.'

'No.' Tamsin finally roused herself. Liz mustn't get up, mustn't draw attention to them both. 'I'm fine, really I am. I just felt a bit odd for a moment, but I'm all right again now.'

'Well, if you're sure,' Liz replied uncertainly, and Tamsin somehow managed a reassuring smile.

How could he do it? The thought spun round in circles inside her head. To take her so much for granted—for now she didn't doubt for a second what the champagne celebration was for. He'd offered her—no, he'd grudgingly allowed her—three days to give her reply, and he hadn't even bothered to wait. So sure of her response, so positive that she had finally seen the folly of daring to put herself between him and his wishes, he was already toasting his success. And with Yolande——

She swallowed, feeling the horrible poison of jealousy, bitter as gall, oozing through every vein in her body, and saw her fingers tighten fiercely on her dessert spoon and fork with the desire to leap to her feet, fall on Yolande and shred her into tiny, unbeautiful pieces.

Like an automaton, she ate up every dusty crumb of the blackcurrant *mille-feuille*, all the time struggling ineffectually to subdue the anger and jealousy that racked her. Stony-faced, she watched as Zak drained his after-lunch brandy, but then, as they stood up and he solicitously escorted Yolande to the door, she thought suddenly, Of course. Thank you, Zak—that's what I must do.

The Manor grounds were deserted. Tamsin roared up the drive, tyres crunching angrily on the gravel, and braked, her front bumper grazing the gleaming rear one of the Range Rover. Well, at least he was back; he'd finally managed to tear himself away from Yolande—unless she was here too. At the thought, her fingers gripped on the ignition key and she all but restarted the engine. Only pride prevented an ignominious retreat.

'On guard, Joss,' she said, over her shoulder—after all, this was enemy territory—and, mounting the wide steps to the pillared entrance, jabbed hard on the doorbell.

She heard footsteps approaching and instantly butterflies of panic swooped wildly in her stomach, but then, 'Why, hello, Tamsin.'

'Good evening, Mrs Meadows. Is Zak—Mr Trenchard in?'

'I think so, dear. Come in.'

As Tamsin stepped into the hall, she caught sight of herself in the oblong gilt mirror. Well, she'd certainly done a good restoration job, she thought wryly. All the way home, her anger had simmered nicely, and, buoyed up on the adrenalin that was pumping through her, she'd gone straight upstairs, where without even a glance in her wardrobe mirror she'd stripped off all her finery, replacing it with her oldest jeans and sweater. After all, she was just a kid, a good little sport, wasn't she, and they didn't wear slinky blouses and tight skirts with slits?

She'd washed her face, then scrubbed at it with a towel until every trace of make-up had disappeared, and finally combed out the feathery curls before knotting her hair into a bun. She surveyed the result with grim satisfaction. Pity about those sun-washed blonde streaks, but otherwise, perfect...

'If you'll just take a seat, dear, I'll go and look for him.'

As the housekeeper went off, Tamsin gazed around the hall, her eyes growing round with astonishment. As long as she could remember, the Manor, deprived for years of money and a woman's loving touch, had been gently decaying. Now, though—she studied the huge Chinese carpet in beige and blue, and the silk wall hangings, in shades of peach, apricot and brown, the soft apricot-white woodwork, the stripped panelling, pale oak where it had always been brown treacle.

Her eyes grew even rounder. No prizes for guessing where the money had come from, and for the first time she was forced reluctantly to a realisation of just how wealthy a man Zak must be.

'He's not in the house, Tamsin.' Mrs Meadows had come back. 'He must be over in the old stables. Shall I take you across?'

'Oh, no, thank you, Mrs Meadows. I remember the way.' Tamsin, tense as a bowstring, now that the moment had come for her confrontation with Zak, got to her feet. 'I'll find him.'

But the cobbled yard was deserted, except for Zak's black stallion which, ears pricked, eyed her with interest over his half-door. She stood indecisively, then saw that the far end of the stable block, which had been ramshackle for years, had had new windows put in, and through them there came a gleam of light. So that was where he was.

She strode across to the brand-new door, put her knuckles to the gleaming scarlet paintwork, but then thought—No. A tentative little knock would give *him* the psychological advantage, and she had every intention of keeping a tight hold of that. So instead, she turned the door-handle and went in.

Whatever she had expected to find, it was not a fully equipped gymnasium. The old, worm-eaten stalls and mangers had been torn out, the walls repanelled in pale pine, and against them stood a fearsome array of what looked like medieval instruments of torture, but which she realised must be exercise machines.

At first she did not see Zak, but then there was a faint creak at the far end and she caught sight of him, sitting with his back supported to an angle of forty-five degrees and pushing backwards and forwards with his legs against a metal bar which was weighed down at each end by massive iron rings.

All the way here, she'd hugged to herself the thought of how she would take him completely by surprise, fall on him and pulverise him into atoms. Now, though, she could only stand watching him, one hand to her throat, all time suspended.

He was wearing only a navy singlet and running shorts, his lean, hard-muscled body merely accentuated by their flimsiness. As he moved, the powerful rhythm forced a little grunt from him each time he thrust hard and his legs straightened against the weighted rod. There was complete silence in the room, except for that regular, guttural sound—and the slow, painful thumping of her heart against her ribs.

But then, for no reason—unless he had heard that tell-tale thump—he glanced over his shoulder.

'Tammy! What the devil are you doing here?'

He stopped abruptly, swung his legs over the edge and stood up. Snatching up the towel which was slung across a chair, he came towards her, wiping his face. Under the fluorescent lights, his tanned body was slicked with sweat and his singlet and shorts clung to him in damp patches, so that it was almost as though he were naked...

Her gaze travelled unwillingly down his chest, his abdomen, across his belly and the faint sprinkle of dark hair which she could discern through the thin material, to his thighs—— Her eyes darkened with shock, and she gave a little gasp at the ugly, puckered scar tissue which ran vertically, ridged and deep, down his left thigh to the knee, and up, disappearing under the edge of his shorts.

Pity welled up in her, but she forced it away. Zak was not a man to welcome pity from anyone. And besides, compassion would undermine her desire for retribution—she could already feel it beginning to slip away from her, and clutched at it desperately.

'Well? What do you want?' He was regarding her impatiently. 'I'm in the middle of my circuit training, and if I stop for long my muscles will seize up.'

'Circuit training?'

'I do a complete round of these contraptions every day. I told you I need to do physio—well, this is it.'

His eyes were challenging her to mention his injuries; she ran the tip of her tongue around her lips, but said nothing.

'I suppose you've come to let me know you've made your mind up. But I gave you three days.' There was that *frisson* of irritation again. 'You needn't have come till tomorrow.'

Tamsin was grateful for that irritation; it had woken her own anger again.

'But you see, Zak, I don't need three days.' She raised her eyes and met his. 'Yes, you're right—I've made my decision.'

'It's taken you long enough to come to your senses, though.' He gave her a smile that was only half teasing, then reached down the short black towelling robe which was hanging from a peg near the door, and slipped it on. 'You're a pigheaded little madam, you know that?'

'Yes, I am, aren't I, Zak?' One part of her was actually savouring this delicious moment. Once and for all, she'd teach him a sharp lesson about taking her for granted. 'Which is, I'm afraid, why the answer is no.'

CHAPTER EIGHT

FOR a moment Zak's fingers stilled on the knot he was tying in the belt of his robe, but then he gave a faint smile.

'That's a pity.' He sounded genuinely regretful. 'I really think the job would suit you fine.'

'I'm not talking about your gracious offer of a job.'

'Oh?' He stared down at her, his eyes narrowing into hard grey bullets of steel. 'And just what the hell are you talking about, then?'

'I'd have thought it was clear enough. I don't want a job from you. I want nothing from you.' That dark, warning flush was erupting along the hard edge of his cheekbone, but Tamsin threw back her head, returning look for look, then said with great deliberation, 'I—am—not—selling—Wethertor—to—you.'

'You little bitch!'

As Zak's hands clenched into fists at his side, she took a step away from him, coming into painful contact with an exercise bicycle. He was looming over her, cutting off her route to the door, and she looked around her wildly, but there was no one here except themselves—no one to stand between her and his fury. She had been so inebriated on her own cocktail of anger and jealousy that she had allowed herself to forget his inevitable reaction. Now, her heart quailed.

'What the hell's got into you? Two days ago you as good as said you were prepared to go along with me!'

'Y-yes, well, that was two days ago,' she said, despising herself for the defensive note in her voice.

'Perhaps you'd be good enough to tell me why?'

'No real reason,' she muttered. 'None that you'd understand, anyway.'

'And that's your final word?'

'Yes.'

'And just what do you intend to do for money?'

The open contempt in his voice made her wince inwardly, but somehow she set her small, soft chin at a pugnacious angle and said, 'Don't worry—I shall manage.'

'I wouldn't be too sure of that, Tamsin,' he replied grimly, and, while she was still trying to decide whether that was a barely veiled threat or not, he went on, 'I suppose you intend to go ahead with your half-baked ideas for camping sites and conifer forests.'

He was losing the battle; he knew he was. That was why he was stooping to insults.

'Yes,' defiantly, 'I shall be putting in planning applications as soon as possible.'

'In that case,' he folded his arms across his chest, 'I must tell you that I shall oppose you all along the line.'

'On what grounds?'

'That campsite, for instance. Think of all the extra traffic that would bring, and you know what the lanes around the village are like—they'd have to be permanently widened to take the type of caravans people expect on a modern site.'

'Well, what about your plans for ex-Army tanks careering all over the countryside?'

'No problem.' She scowled up at him, hating his arrogant self-assurance. 'They'll be confined to the old airfield, and the roads that side are plenty wide enough to get them there—or if not, I shall just have to airlift them in.'

'We'll see,' she said stubbornly. 'My schemes have at least as much chance of getting approved as yours.'

'I wouldn't be too sure of that.' Zak gave her a slow, calculating look. 'Just how many friends have you got on the planning committee?'

'Why, none, of course. Oh——' Her jaw sagged, as the import of his words hit her.

'Exactly. Now you know why my plans are going through, and I can say with some conviction that yours won't.'

All the confidence, that she'd only half believed in anyway, was shrivelling away, punctured by Zak's ruthless attack, into a tight little ball of misery in her chest, but she mustn't let him see that. He was so hard himself, harder even than the granite column of Luscombe Man, that he would pounce on the slightest sign of weakness. She half turned to go.

'Oh, but I haven't finished yet, Tamsin.' His silky tone stopped her in her tracks.

'W-what do you mean?' She couldn't manage quite to meet his eye.

'I hear you've been having problems meeting your feed bills.'

'How—how did you know that?' The words were jerked out of her and she felt herself colour with angry humiliation. 'You've been snooping into my private affairs!'

'Oh, I wouldn't say that. It's just that Bert Fallowes, in case you've forgotten, as well as being your supplier, is still one of our tenants, and anything that affects *his* cash flow—a reluctant payer, for instance——' he went smoothly on over her little gasp of mingled outrage and entreaty '—is going to be of great interest to me.'

So that was why Bert, so out of character, had been pressurising her. He'd had this—this swine on his back! Impotent rage was taking her over and her fingers curled into claws with the desire to launch herself at Zak, raking his face.

Instead, she hunched her shoulders and turned away again, but his cold voice pursued her remorselessly, the words falling into the air between them like chips of ice.

'And when you do come crawling to me, honey, begging me on your knees to buy, the offer I made two days ago will be off. I'll give you the current market price—if you're lucky. Not one penny more.'

Tamsin's self-control, stretched like a rubber band, finally snapped. Whirling round, she flung herself on him, her hands reaching upwards to tear that supercilious smile off his face.

He'd obviously thought that he had so ground her down that she would only be able to creep away like a wounded animal, and her attack momentarily knocked him off balance. He staggered back against the wall, but then seized her by the wrists, holding her away from him at arm's length.

'L-let me go, you bastard!' Sobbing for breath, she could scarcely get the words out, and when his only response was to grip her more tightly she aimed a vicious kick at his ankle.

'Tammy, stop it, you idiot, or you'll hurt yourself.'

He was laughing openly at her now, and that laugh, coupled with the certainty that he was merely containing her assault, added to her rage. All her struggles were having about as much effect on that hard body as though she were a small bird fluttering helplessly in his grasp, and he was actually enjoying himself immensely—she knew that.

'Will you let me go?'

She aimed another kick, the toe of her trainer catching him full on the shin. This time he winced and swore, and she felt his grip slacken momentarily, enough for her to draw her right arm free and aim a punch at his chin. But he warded off her small fist with the side of his hand, and before she could throw another right hook he had seized her again, by the shoulders this time.

'Stop it, you little spitfire, or I'll really set about you,' though he was still laughing.

'Good,' she panted, aiming another flailing blow. 'That's what you've been longing to do ever since we first met in the wood, isn't it? Come on, then, beat me up, you great bully!'

But instead he wrapped his arms tightly around her, pulling her to him and pinioning her so hard against him that she felt the breath being squeezed out of her body until her lungs all but squeaked.

In another second he would subdue her completely. With her last strength, she put her hands against his chest and levered herself away from him. Wriggling free from under his arms, she turned to make her escape, all thought of fight swamped by the instinct for self-preservation.

'Oh, no, you don't!'

Zak seized her again, swinging her round by the shoulders to face him. He was still laughing at her, that maddening laugh, and she glowered up at him through the tangle of hair which, torn free from its precarious knot, was tumbling over her face and shoulders.

But then the laugh faded abruptly.

'Tammy?' He was staring down at her dazedly, as though he had never set eyes on her before.

'Y-yes?'

There was something in his eyes which she could not understand, but which made her heart, already beating fast, lurch erratically against her ribcage.

'Tammy,' he said again, that same note, almost of wonderment, in his voice.

Then, as she ceased to breathe altogether, slowly, with infinite slowness, his eyes on her face, he drew her to him. Putting his thumb under her chin, he gently tilted her face to his, then his lips came down to meet hers.

She was imagining this, she had to be—it wasn't happening. And yet she could feel his mouth, warm and soft against hers, and she closed her eyes, surrendering to the moment. Encircled by his arms, she was filled with a multitude of heady sensations: the smoothness of his lips, the rasp of his chin, the crisp thick hair at his nape, where half consciously her fingers had clutched, the mingled aroma of spicy sandalwood and the musky scent of male sweat, and, as his robe came unknotted, through the silky vest and shorts she could feel the surging power of that strong masculine body.

Never in her life had she experienced feelings like this, engulfing her with joy, fear, and a wild elation. She heard herself give a little moan, then felt, as if in answer, Zak's tongue part her lips, thrusting in and filling not just her mouth but her whole body with a sweet intoxication that made her senses spin, so that she clung to him.

This was what she had dreamed of, all her life it seemed, long before she was old enough to have had such dreams...when she and Zak and Sarah——

Sarah! Was this how he had kissed her too? And not only Sarah, but Yolande? On the thought, her eyes flew open and she jerked back her head.

'Stop it, Zak.'

She could barely get the words out, and, gulping for air, felt light-headed, as though she had just surfaced from a too-long underwater swim. His grip loosened fractionally and he drew back as well. He too was breathing hard, his chest rising and falling, and as he frowned down at her as though he hardly saw her she dragged the back of her hand across her mouth, to wipe away all traces of his lips.

At her gesture his face hardened. 'What's the matter?'

'Did she let you down, then?'

'She? What the hell are you talking about?'

'Didn't she come up trumps in bed for you?' The pain and self-anger goaded it out of her.

'Don't be crude, Tammy. It doesn't suit you.' He had recovered his composure completely now— much quicker than she had—and the old coldness was back. 'And what the devil do you mean?'

At his expression she bit her lip, but it was too late now to retract the words. 'You and Yolande, that's what I mean.'

'Me and Yolande?' Zak was staring down at her blankly. 'You're off your tiny head!'

'I was there, Zak—in the restaurant. I saw you.'

He gaped at her. 'Good Lord! So it *was* you. I thought there was something familiar about that tarted-up little bint——'

'How dare you?' Tamsin's bosom swelled with outraged pride. 'And anyway, I'm amazed, the way you were all over her, you could even notice anybody else.'

He was still holding her by one arm, but she wrenched it away. 'I'll go now—leave you to break the sad news to her.'

'What do you mean by that?'

'Just that your little champagne celebration was a fraction premature. You were so sure of yourself, weren't you—so sure that you'd finally wheedled me round?'

'Now look.' He was clearly only just managing to rein himself in. 'Not that it's any business of yours, but whatever you saw—or thought you saw—you've got it all wrong. We *were* celebrating—yes. But not the downfall of one pig-headed little——' He bit off the word and went on, 'Yolande has agreed to invest a substantial sum in Trenchard Enterprises and we'd just been to my solicitors to sign the contract.'

'Oh.' Tamsin felt herself deflate a little.

'Yolande's a very shrewd businesswoman.' Unlike some people not a million miles away, was the clear meaning. 'She can see the potential for excellent returns—with or without your co-operation.' He shot her an unpleasant look. 'But that's all it is— a business relationship. After what sounds like a messy marriage and an even messier divorce, she is definitely off men—for good, I'd say, and that suits me. From my experience, business and—pleasure don't mix!'

Tamsin looked at him, nonplussed. He was doing it again, cutting the ground from under her feet, and if she allowed herself to weaken any more he would press home his advantage and drive her to total defeat.

'Well, anyway,' she said, struggling to drag her defensive rags around her, 'that was no reason for you to think you could—manhandle me.' But at the memory of that embrace, she felt herself flush, and hurried on, 'It was just stage three in your softening-up process, wasn't it? Stage one, helping me with the lambing, stage two, taking me up in your balloon—just the kind of treat to turn the head of a simple kid like me.'

He opened his mouth to interrupt, but she swept on, 'And now, stage three, a kiss and a cuddle and I'm putty in your hands.' In spite of herself, there was a tremor in her voice and she drew a long, shuddering breath to try to steady it. 'I should have tumbled to it earlier, of course—after all, I've known you all my life, and we both know, don't we, just what a calculating swine you are?'

For a moment the words hung perilously in the air between them. But then his lip curled contemptuously. 'Think what you like. I've already wasted more than enough time on you for one evening. See yourself out—I'm going to have a shower.'

He snatched up the towel, turned his back and walked away. The swing door at the far end banged behind him, and as Tamsin stood, frozen, she heard the sound of gushing water. She roused herself with an effort and went slowly out of the room.

CHAPTER NINE

TAMSIN piled the last home-made walnut biscuits on to a plate. Rolls, sandwiches, buttered scones, tea—yes, everything was ready, even though the students wouldn't have finished their war game for a couple of hours at least. There was time for her to have a sit-down, but that meant there was also time for her to think, and that was something she'd tried by every means to avoid over the last couple of days.

Perhaps she could move the old trestle-tables into the orchard. It was far too lovely a day for them to want to come indoors, and besides, she'd hardly squash them all in here. Forty of them—her largest group so far—and they'd seemed happy enough to pay the eighty pounds she'd tentatively suggested. Peanuts by Zak's standards, of course—she could imagine him curling his lip in sneering contempt—but really the war games were beginning to take off—the one bright spot in an otherwise bleak landscape . . .

But as she opened the kitchen door, she stopped dead. They were coming back across the yard, trailing in a forlorn little draggle, and as she watched, Simon, the third-year engineering student who organised the group's outings, cut the heads off a clump of nettles with a vicious swipe of his rifle butt.

'What's wrong?' Tamsin was hurrying to meet them. 'Is—is someone hurt?'

'Ask that creep Brian.' Simon jerked a thumb in the direction of another student, who was walking on his own. 'I wish to God we'd never brought him.' And he slumped down on to the stone platform that had once been used for the milk churns.

Tamsin looked round in puzzlement at the despondent faces. 'Look, I'm sorry if you've had your day spoilt.'

'You'll be sorrier still soon, I'm afraid, Tamsin.' He pulled a rueful face. 'I know these war games are important to you, and——'

His voice tailed away, and Tamsin, after a long look at him, marched up to the other young man and demanded bluntly, 'What's wrong, Brian?'

'Ah, Tamsin, I've got some marvellous news for you.' He beamed down at her from behind his pebble glasses, seemingly oblivious to the chorus of groans that greeted his words. 'Do you realise that in your wood there's a flourishing colony of *spiranthes aestivalis*?'

'What?' She stared at him uncomprehendingly. 'What on earth are you talking about?'

'*Spiranthes aestivalis*—Summer Lady's Tresses,' he added, with the patient air of one long used to dealing with fools. 'Look, come with me and I'll show you. They're growing all along the edge of the stream.'

Light dawned. 'Oh, you mean those little white orchids. I've often wondered what they were. Summer Lady's Tresses—what a lovely name——'

'Of course, I had to stop the game, you understand.'

'Stop the game?' she repeated, a feeling of vague disquiet creeping over her.

'Oh, yes. We can't risk them being harmed in any way.'

'But they aren't that special—there are some much prettier orchids in the pasture over there. Lovely mauve ones——'

'*Dactylorhiza praetermissa*, you mean?' Brian was scornfully dismissive. 'Oh, you can see them anywhere. But, Tamsin, *spiranthes aestivalis*— they're different. They've been thought to be extinct for years, yet here you've got them growing— maybe the last in England!'

'Well, that's marvellous.' Tamsin was impressed—and a little proud. 'But I still don't see——'

'Of course, we shall have to get things moving straight away—inform the Nature Conservancy Council and put in for an SSSI.'

'What's that?' As she looked blankly at him, the vague disquiet became definite unease.

'A Site of Special Scientific Interest. And I have to inform you,' Brian already had the officious tone of the civil servant he would doubtless be in a few years, 'that I'm placing a preliminary order on Luscombe Wood, to take immediate effect.'

'What the nerk means, Tamsin,' Simon chipped in sourly as she stood, bereft of speech, 'is that, as of now, your war games are off.'

'B-but that's impossible!'

Dazed, she could only look from one to the other, feeling the frightening chill creep through her. The war games off? But it was precisely that regular income which was keeping her petty cash book at all bearable to look at. Without them—— She swallowed.

'Don't be offended, Brian, but there's no chance you could be wrong, is there?'

'Oh, no.' He shook his head, bridling slightly, and dug out a small book from his pocket. 'I've checked in my Keble Martin—there's no error, I assure you.'

'Well, in that case——' Tamsin stopped, biting her lip as the enormity of what was happening at last hit home, but then she managed a bright smile '—well, in that case, come and have something to eat, all of you. And of course, there'll be no charge for today. No,' as they tried to protest, 'after all, you've had the expense of hiring the coach for nothing.'

The trouble with grand gestures, though, she reflected, as she made tea in the kitchen a few minutes later, was that they might be very satisfying to make, but they usually cost money...

'Here, Joss.'

As the dog delicately took the scone from her and gulped it down Tamsin gave a little sigh. Most of the students had been too upset—for her, not themselves—to eat much, so when they had gone she had grimly packed her old freezer chock-full of ham rolls, cheese sandwiches and buttered scones.

But then, too restive to stay in the house, she'd whistled up Joss and come striding over the moor, veering away whenever she saw groups of weekend walkers. She'd gone first to the wood, where she'd stood for several minutes staring down at those pale, insignificant-looking little flower spikes. If only she'd brought a trowel with her—she might even be able to persuade that wretched Brian that he'd been dreaming...

But she'd pushed the unworthy thought away and left the wood, to wander across the moor until she came, as subconsciously she'd known she would, to the Secret Valley. She hadn't been here for years, not since Zak had gone away that second time— no, since before that, when he and Sarah had taken to riding off alone and she would deliberately turn her old pony in the opposite direction, so that she wouldn't meet up with them.

And yet, although Sarah was dead, and Tamsin and Zak were so altered, here nothing had changed. She had followed the river from rock pool to rock pool, then, where the rowan tree still hung over the lip of the waterfall, she'd scrambled down alongside it to huddle under the lee of the rock, shivering slightly in the thin drizzle which had set in after the lovely morning.

At first, her thoughts were all but drowned out by the constant roar of the falls into the deep pool beside her, but gradually they came sneaking back. How could she possibly keep going now, with the loss of the games? She'd have no option but to give in ignominiously to Zak. Of course, the loss of the wood would make a dent in his own plans, but, knowing him as she did, that wouldn't stop him taking over all her land. He was so determined to get his own way...

But no, she would not give in. She was committed now—she'd given him her answer, and pride would not allow her to change her mind. Just a few days ago, she'd thought she couldn't bear to stay at Wethertor, loving Zak, but she couldn't possibly remain in love with a man like him for long—could she? And so...

Round and round her thoughts went, like buzzing flies—until she realised that Joss was no longer beside her.

'Joss?' She got to her feet, turning up her collar against the steady rain. 'Joss, where are you?' She whistled, and heard a faint bark from downstream.

Below the falls the valley deepened abruptly to a gorge where the shallow, pretty stream became a torrent as it was forced into a narrowing bottleneck of rock. This was a horrible place, dark and overhung, and ever since she could remember, far more than any of the dangerous, pony-swallowing mires on the moor, it had terrified her. Now, as she stumbled along, she felt the old childish fear grip her.

At the very narrowest point, where the river was only five feet wide, the far side almost disappeared under a wall of solid rock. There was just a narrow ledge, lower than the bank where she stood—an invitingly easy jump from her side, but an upward leap over a thirty-foot depth of swirling green water from the other. Dead Man's Step, the locals called it, with good reason, and Tamsin saw now that Joss was on that far side, running back and forth on the ledge.

As he saw her, he crouched as though to spring.

'*No*, Joss—stay!'

Tamsin heard herself cry out, thin and high against the tumbling waters, then, deliberately, before the sick fear that was clutching her stomach could paralyse her completely, she leapt.

Dimly, she felt the pain as her left hand grazed the rock, but then she crouched down beside Joss, who was frenziedly licking her, and drew him back away from the spray. Her eye measured the gap, less than the width of the porch at home, and yet...

'It's all right, boy. Someone will come,' she said reassuringly to both of them. But this was a remote spot at the best of times, and in heavy rain... Suppose no one came tonight? Suppose no one came until tomorrow? Suppose no one came until it was too late? I must not panic, she whispered to herself, and swallowed down the hard, tight lump which had settled in her chest and was threatening to explode at any moment into full-blown hysterical terror.

Hugging Joss to her, so that his body heat very slightly warmed her own chilled body, she tried not to look at the water eddying beneath her and, surely, as the rain continued, minute by minute rising further up towards the lip of the rock. Instead, to distract herself from that creeping tide, she peered through her tangled fringe at her watch. Seven o'clock. Soon it would be dark. No one would come. Hot, weak tears stung her cold eyes and she blinked them away.

'Someone will come, I promise.' She said the words aloud.

Until then, she would count the time: sixty seconds make one minute, sixty minutes make one hour... She managed to focus on her watch again and almost wept with disappointment to see the hands pointing to seven-ten.

The toes on one foot felt even colder and, when she wriggled them, wet. Lifting her head from where it lay against the cliff face, she saw that that creeping tide, edged now with a grey frill of froth, had spilled over the lip of rock and reached the toe of that trainer. She stared down at it for a moment with dull eyes, then drew both feet back with a shudder of sick fear, squeezing them into her thighs.

As she moved, her arm brushed against something in her anorak pocket and she took out the paper bag which contained the last scone. It seemed a hundred years since she'd made them. Joss was sniffing at it, so she broke it down the middle, gave him one half and nibbled a little from the other. But the crumbs turned to choking ashes in her mouth, and she held the rest out to him. He ate it, then whined and shifted his forepaws restlessly.

'It's all right, boy. We're going home soon,' she said, in a high, childish voice.

The rush of water was having a hypnotic effect on her, making her drowsy, so that she longed to sleep. But she had to keep awake. Count those pieces of gravel in front of her feet. One—two—three—four. The furthest pebble, caught up by a little surge of water, rolled round and round in the eddy, then, as she watched in fascinated horror, it was sucked into the river.

Count the rowan trees on the opposite bank. She peered through the driving spears of rain. One—two——

'Tammy!'

——three—four——

'Tammy! Where are you?'

She frowned and shook her head slightly, as the insistent shout broke the rhythm of her counting. But then—could it be?

'Zak!'

She scrambled to her feet, then, as she almost overbalanced, sank back down again. She was hallucinating, she must be; she squeezed her eyes tight shut, then reopened them and saw, through the rain and the dusk, a figure coming down the track on a black horse.

He reined in the horse hard as he saw her, swung himself down from the saddle, flicked the bridle over a low-hanging branch, and came on down the bank.

'Zak.' The name came out as a little sob.

'Stay there.' His voice cut through the roar of water and Joss's excited barks. Then, as she moved, as though to get to her feet again, 'No. Stay there, for heaven's sake!'

He came down to the very edge, opposite her. He was limping; she'd forgotten his limp. He mustn't jump—he'd never make it, he'd be swept away, and then what would she have to live for?

'No—don't!' She tried to shout, but her tongue was frozen to the roof of her mouth, and before she could try again he had leapt the chasm. As he landed, right beside her, she saw him wince with pain, but then he was kneeling over her, gripping her by the shoulders.

'Oh, God, Tammy, are you all right?' She still could barely hear him above the cascading waters.

'I——' she began, but then the shock of having him here, holding her, was too much. The tension snapped and, as her mouth turned down, she put her hand up to her wet face and began to cry, not softly but loudly, noisily, like a child.

'Oh, don't, Tam.'

Zak drew her to him, making soothing noises as though she really were a child, until at last the tears stopped. He held her away from him a fraction.

'All right?'

When she nodded he got up, pulling her up with him but still keeping her in the crook of his arm, sheltered against his body. He glanced down and grimaced, and when she followed his eyes she saw that the froth-edged tide had just surged over on to one of his riding boots. But he grinned down at her reassuringly.

'I don't think it's too healthy here, so let's go, shall we?'

She didn't want to jump. Every fibre of her screamed out *No*, but she couldn't let Zak see what a miserable little coward she was, so, gulping down the panic, she forced herself to face the water.

'*No*—this way!'

Zak shouted in her ear and, snatching at her wet hand, he towed her along the ledge towards its narrowest point, then turned to her. The rain was streaming down his face, plastering his black hair to his skull like a helmet.

'Now, up here,' he commanded, but when she followed the direction of his jabbing finger, she saw a vertical cleft in the rock face above them.

'No!' Horrified, she shrank back. 'No, I can't!'

But he grabbed hold of her, shaking her by the shoulders.

'*Yes*. You must. I'll be right behind you if you slip.' So they would both of them hurtle into the river.

'Joss—I won't leave him.'

'You bloody well will!' He was getting angry, and she could never bear Zak's anger. 'And anyway, where you go, he'll follow. Now—move!' And he pushed her roughly towards the cleft.

All her life, Tamsin would never forget that climb. Barely forty feet and yet so sheer, and the fissure so narrow that she could scarcely squeeze through, her hands clawing for finger-holds on the tussocks of rough grass and heather growing directly out of the rock. Several times her toes scrabbled frantically for purchase, and each time, somehow, Zak's hands found a nick in the rock for them to fasten on.

Once she half turned, but he yelled out, '*No*— don't look round!' So she heaved herself up past the final obstruction and fell forward on her face across the tangled roots of a hawthorn bush on to level ground.

She lay on the wet grass, her breath thundering in her ears, and dimly felt Zak collapse beside her, one arm across her, then Joss was licking her hand.

Gradually, their harsh breathing subsided and Zak rolled over to face her. Their eyes were very close together, but after one glance Tamsin couldn't meet his gaze.

'OK now?' he asked softly, lifting a last tear from her cheek with his little finger.

'Mmm.' She hardly had the strength to nod. 'Thank you, Zak—for saving my life. If I'd been stuck there all night——' Her voice shook, and the realisation of what had so nearly happened made her tremble in every limb.

'Oh, Tam, don't look like that,' he said harshly, and gathered her to him. But then, just as roughly, he pushed her away and abruptly sat up.

'How the hell did you get yourself into that mess, anyway? If I've told you once not to go to the Step, I've told you a hundred times.'

Yes, but that was years ago—when you could order me around like an older brother . . .

'Well, Joss went across and——'

'I might have known he'd have something to do with it! And of course you had to follow him.' He shook his head in exasperation. 'It really was a stupid, idiotic thing to do.'

'I couldn't just leave him there, could I?' Her nerves, raw already, were smarting under his attack. 'And anyway, you must have been there before, to know all about that way out.'

'Yes, well, that's different.'

'I don't see why—and I suppose you'll be telling me next that it's time I grew up, that I'm still just a silly kid.'

'Oh, no, Tammy, I shan't tell you that—ever again.'

There was a hint of sadness—or regret, even—in his tone, but then he said briskly, 'Come on. Time we were moving—you must be soaked to the skin.' But when he got up stiffly, holding out his hands to her, she scrambled to her feet unaided.

'We'll need to get back to where the river widens out,' he said. 'We can cross it at the stepping-stones, then collect Satan—my horse,' he added, with a quirk of his mouth as she looked quickly up at him.

Once they were across the river, Tamsin waited, huddled under a tree with Joss, while Zak fetched the horse. She was watching him ride slowly back to her, picking his way among the granite boulders, when all at once, without warning, a terrible longing took possession of her, a longing to hold him to her, to have him love her——

'Are you aiming on sitting there all night?' Zak's acid tone roused her abruptly from her bitter-sweet little dream.

He put out a hand and, as he swung her into the saddle in front of him, the big horse pranced sideways, then steadied. Zak whistled to Joss, then, pulling on the bridle, turned Satan's head for home.

'W-what a coincidence—your coming to the Step, I mean.'

Tamsin knew that her voice was strained and unnatural but, sitting there, perched in front of Zak, she was conscious only of his arms around her, his warm breath curling round her neck, scorching the cold skin.

'No coincidence. I'd just got back from a training session with my men when Matt rang. He was worried out of his wits—he knew you were out on the moor somewhere, and wondered if I'd seen you.'

'But it was still lucky that you found me.'

'Not entirely.' She could almost hear the wry little smile. 'I somehow guessed that you'd headed for the Secret Valley, and then I just followed the stream down.'

He moved one arm slightly to steer the horse, and it lay casually along the outside of her thigh. As little rivulets of sensation started rippling out from under the pressure of that hand, every muscle in her body tensed. But as she edged forward a little, Zak, catching the surreptitious movement, said caustically, 'Don't worry—I'm not going to demand recompense.'

'R-recompense?' Tamsin was staring straight ahead.

'Yes, you know. Your life—and Joss's, of course—in exchange for the farm. So you needn't sit there like a stiff little ramrod.'

Next second, he had slid his free arm across her stomach and drawn her closer to him. Well, at least he'd misunderstood her reaction, she thought, even if Wethertor was still firmly in his sights, and so, after resisting for a moment longer, she let herself go, sinking into the comforting shelter of his body. She felt him open his windproof jacket and as he drew it round her she leaned back, allowing her eyes to close.

CHAPTER TEN

'COME ON—down you get!'

Tamsin roused, to find that Zak was lifting her down from the saddle. It was quite dark, apart from a light coming from——

Her eyes widened with alarm. 'What have you brought me here for?'

'I suppose you'd rather go back to a cold, dark, *lonely* farmhouse?' he said roughly. 'Well, sorry. You're staying at the Manor tonight, just to make sure there are no ill-effects. Though why I bother——' as she struggled, in spite of the miasma of fatigue, to look stubbornly determined '—is beyond me.'

And, picking her up, he carried her up the steps into the warmth of the hall and dumped her on to a chair. She'd sat here, in this very chair, just the other evening, before she'd found him in the old stables, and before——

'Why, Tamsin, whatever's the matter?' The housekeeper had come bustling out of the kitchen, and was staring at her in alarm.

'She's all right, Mrs Meadows.' Zak smiled at the woman reassuringly, then added firmly, 'I can manage, thanks. If you'll just take Joss through to the kitchen and put him by the fire, then organise a hot drink—and something to eat.'

And after one doubtful look at the girl, still hunched in the chair, Mrs Meadows retreated, leading Joss warily by the collar, and Zak turned back to Tamsin.

'Now, let's have a look at you.' He was still addressing her in that curt, offhand tone. 'A hot bath first, I think, some dry clothes, and then food.'

Tamsin eyed him resentfully, about to protest vigorously that she wanted no such thing, but somehow she was up the stairs, along a passage, and Zak was opening a door. She blinked. Surely the main bathroom at the Manor had always been a huge, dingy affair, with an old-fashioned bath and, along the ceiling, pipes that clanked horribly whenever you turned on the taps?

This bathroom was completely different. True, the massive old mahogany-clawed bath was still there, but now it rubbed shoulders with a modern, honey-coloured suite with gold-plated taps, a luxurious, glass-enclosed shower cabinet, and a range of units topped with creamy brown marble. And Zak had only been back a few short weeks. His vitality, his energy—it was almost frightening...

She stood watching, a little shyly, as he started running hot water, laying out towels and a new tablet of soap—the sandalwood which he used himself, to judge by that faint musky fragrance which was always on his skin.

'Right.' He glanced round the room with a nod of satisfaction. 'Take as long as you like. I'll give Matt a ring—tell him I've found the waif,' just for a moment, as he looked at her, his hard face softened, but then that softness was gone, 'rub down Satan, then have a bath myself. Oh, don't worry,' as her eyes shot to him, 'not here—though there's plenty of room. I've got my own bathroom. So, into the water with you.'

When she still hesitated, one hand to her anorak zipper, he pushed her fingers aside with an irritated exclamation. But as his hand brushed hers, she winced and, glancing down, saw with astonishment that her palm was scored across with scratches and from one deeper cut the blood had oozed, then dried.

Zak took her hand and stared down at it, his lips tight, but all he said, in a cold, remote voice, was, 'You've got some shards of rock in it. I'll see to them later.' And turning on his heel, he went out of the room.

Tamsin, cocooned in blissfully hot water, heard the knock, and before she had time to remember that she hadn't locked the door and shout, 'No, don't come in,' it opened, Zak's voice said, 'You can wear these,' a hand came in, dumped a heap of clothes on the floor, and then withdrew. The door-handle reclosed and Tamsin, realising that she was clutching the sponge between her fingers as though it were a lifeline, let it flop back into the water and then lay, watching the slow trail of bubbles as it sank.

But the interruption had jerked her out of that rosy haze into reality. Here she was at the Manor—alien territory, and Zak her enemy—although to-night, after all he'd done for her, it was harder than

ever to see him that way. And it was here, just a
few nights ago, that he'd taken her in his arms and
kissed her—— She closed her eyes as the recollection of that kiss swept through her again.

But there must be no repetition of that scene.
She mustn't allow it—for who could tell what might
happen if Zak kissed her once more, so that her
knees began to turn to water and that terrifying
sensation swept through her again.

The water was getting cold. She hauled herself
out and, rather soberly, began drying herself. When
she lifted the pile of clothes which Zak had dropped
in, she saw a navy towelling robe and cream
pyjamas, far too large for her—they were his, presumably. She stared at them resentfully; there were
plenty of women in the house, weren't there, that
he could have borrowed from? She wouldn't put
them on. But when she snatched up her sweater
and jeans, and felt the sodden fabric squelch in her
fingers, she reluctantly gave in.

Mrs Meadows was waiting for her in the hall.
'Ah, good, Tamsin. You've got your dirty clothes.'
She held out her hands. 'If you'll just let me have
them, Mr Trenchard said I was to wash and dry
them for you.'

'Oh, there's no need, Mrs Meadows, thank you.'
Tamsin clutched the bundle firmly to her bosom,
like a soggy talisman against ill-luck.

'Well, if you're sure——' The housekeeper obviously wasn't. 'He did say——'

'Quite sure, thank you. I'll just dry them by the fire.' Tamsin smiled brightly and allowed herself to be escorted into the sitting-room.

Zak had changed into a pale yellow lambswool sweater and black cords. He was standing at the far end of the room, his head propped on one elbow on the Adam mantelpiece, gazing moodily down into the red-gold heart of the log fire. There was a forbidding, withdrawn quality about him which made her shrink back from breaking into his train of thought, but he had heard them come in and was already turning.

As he came across to them, he caught sight of the clothes in Tamsin's arms and said with a frown, 'I thought I said these were to be washed, Mrs Meadows.'

'No, it's all right, Zak,' Tamsin put in hastily. 'I can dry them off in here. I'm going home soon, so——'

'Here you are.' And before she could draw back, he had neatly removed the bundle from her clutching fingers and handed it to the housekeeper, standing just behind her. 'If you'll just see to them now.'

'Very good, Mr Trenchard.'

Tamsin opened her mouth to argue, but then, realising that behind the professional façade the woman's ears were almost twitching with the effort to pick up any undercurrents between her and Zak, she gave her another dazzling smile. 'Thank you, Mrs Meadows. It's very kind of you.'

'Oh—and is the guest suite ready for Miss Westmacott?'

'Yes, sir. Mary's prepared it.'

'Good. You can bring the supper in as soon as you're ready.'

The moment they were alone, Tamsin's smile faded and she said determinedly, 'I'm not staying, Zak. I'll have something to eat, but then I'm going home.'

'In that get-up?' He looked down at her, taking in the pyjamas, rolled up at the ankles and pushed back from her slim wrists, and the gown, so large that it hung off her shoulders. 'Sorry, but I'm not turning out *again*——' he gave her a meaningful look '—on a night like this. So for heaven's sake, Tammy,' absently, he lifted up the collar of the robe, where it was sliding down her shoulder, and adjusted it, his finger brushing across her neck, 'come over here and get warm.'

'I——' she began, but he seized her hand, propelled her across to the sofa and gave her a little push down into it.

As he picked up the brass poker and began prodding at the logs, she stared at him, her eyes troubled. One touch—that was all it had been. A casual brush of his warm, strong fingers on her neck, and she could feel the treacherous ache of longing uncurling itself inside her again.

Zak gave the logs a final prod, which sent a golden shower of sparks fizzing into the chimney, then turned to her. He must have caught something in her face, though she had hastily wiped it clean of all expression, for he said, 'What's the matter now?'

His tone was brusque—maybe he wasn't quite so perfectly at ease as he'd seemed. But that thought, far from reassuring her, only made her even more tense.

'I—I——' Tamsin looked away from those penetrating grey eyes, thought wildly, then said, 'It's my hand.' She wasn't lying; even after the bath, her palm was still sore. 'But it'll be all right,' she added, too late, as he squatted down in front of her and took her hand.

He turned it over, letting it lie in his, then bent over it. That head, so close to hers, the black hair, turning up into tiny half-curls round his ears where it was still slightly damp from his bath . . . The ache inside her suddenly turned into a vicious, stabbing pain that brought tears to her eyes.

Glancing up, he said, 'Sorry—did I hurt you?'

'No. Well, not much,' she amended. After all, it was far better if he believed that.

'Hmm. Well, I think the bath got all the bits of dirt out. I'll fetch some antiseptic cream.' And this time she didn't even try to protest.

When he had gone, she leaned back into the squashy sofa and, as much to subdue her still quivering nerves as out of curiosity, she allowed her eyes to travel round the beautifully proportioned room. Here, as in the other parts of the house she had seen, Zak's miraculous transformation act was in evidence. Soft, deep-pile carpet in rose and green, tones which were echoed in the full-length curtains

and the loose covers of the suite and which set off
the gleaming antique mahogany chests and side-
tables.

'You approve, I trust?'

She jumped as Zak's voice came from just behind
her.

'Oh, yes, it's lovely.'

'You recognise some of the pieces, of course.
That Sheraton cabinet there, for instance—it used
to house my mother's china, remember?'

Tamsin glanced up at him sharply. This was the
very first time that she had heard him speak of his
mother since she had left, but his face was totally
expressionless. He dropped down on to the sofa
beside her, unscrewed the tube of ointment and,
taking a firm grip on her hand, began smearing on
the cream.

'To be honest,' he remarked, 'although I know
it's a heretical statement in a room like this, my
taste in furniture runs more to modern
Scandinavian.'

Yes, it would, she thought. The teak and black
leather, the clean, vigorous lines would suit you
perfectly. She watched him unroll some gauze, cut
it, form it into a pad, then place it on her palm,
finally fixing it into place with a length of bandage.
How skilful he was; he did everything with that
same beautiful, economical efficiency of
movement, which was a kind of elegance. She
couldn't imagine him ever being awkward or
clumsy—except with his limp, of course, and the
exercises would surely ease that in time. Otherwise

he had the innate grace of the natural athlete in every action of his body—whether he was controlling a spirited stallion, or coaxing life into a newborn lamb. Probably he made love with that same blend of strength and delicacy——

Horrified, she caught up her thoughts, but he must have felt the slight *frisson* which quivered inside her, for he glanced up quickly. Before he could speak, though, there was a knock and Mrs Meadows came in with a tray loaded with two steaming bowls of cream of watercress soup, cold meats, salad, rolls and butter.

She set it down on a coffee-table near them, then smiled kindly at Tamsin. 'Feeling better now, dear? Oh, and you're not to worry about Joss.' Tamsin gave a guilty start. In fact, she realised, appalled, she hadn't given her dog a single thought since she had arrived at the Manor. 'Mary's fed him and now he's settled down on a rug by the kitchen fire.'

'Thank you, Mrs Meadows. You're spoiling both of us.'

'Oh, and Mr Trenchard—I nearly forgot, in all the bother—Mrs Davies rang earlier. She was in a bit of a state—something about the fairy lights for the dance tomorrow.'

Zak rolled his eyes and gave a dramatic sigh. 'Oh, lord, I'm beginning to regret the whole thing. All right, I'll give her a quick call now.'

He followed the housekeeper out of the room and moments later Tamsin heard his voice in the hall. An apology—laughter—protestations—hesitation, then agreement, though reluctant, surely—then a long, rather one-sided conversation, nearly all from Mrs Davies' end, Zak's voice smoothly polite, but she could sense the growing irritation and hoped that the vicar's wife could not also discern it.

Eventually he came back, pulling a face; he flopped down in the armchair facing her and expelled a long breath. He'd obviously been running his hand through his hair, for it looked quite ruffled.

'Sorry about that. You should have started.'

He pulled the table across and handed her one of the bowls of soup. As she took it, Tamsin's curiosity got the better of her.

'Problems?'

Zak seemed about to say something, but then changed his mind. 'Not really. She was just asking a favour, that's all.'

'But what's this dance all about?' she persisted.

'What's this dance?' He rolled his eyes again. 'Where have you *been* the last few weeks, for God's sake? Haven't you seen the posters everywhere?'

'I've been very busy,' she said, with a touch of asperity in her voice.

'OK, OK.' He held up a placatory hand. 'Anyway, it's the May Day dance, of course—we're holding it here at the Manor, instead of the village hall.'

'*What?*' Soup spilled from her astonished spoon.

'Why not? After all, it always used to be here, didn't it?'

'Well—yes,' she said slowly, picking her words with care. 'But not for years.'

'All right. I know Dad could never be bothered with it, but—well, let's just say that when Mrs Davies asked me, I couldn't resist playing the gracious Lord of the Manor, just for once.' Zak shot her a disarming smile. 'Anyway, the dance is to be in the old ballroom, if wet, or out there on the lawn,' he gestured past the closed curtains, 'if dry—and she assures me that it will be.' He paused. 'You're coming, I hope?'

'Well, I-I'm not sure.' In fact, she hadn't been to the dance since Sarah had left, and she certainly wouldn't this year, if it was to be held here.

'Oh, do come.' He gave her a slanted smile. 'In my new-found role as Lord of Luscombe, I'll even open the dancing with you.'

'No—you can't possibly do that.' Tamsin shook her head firmly. 'You know that the Stag King always does that with the Maid.'

'Ah yes, of course—I'd forgotten,' he said blandly. 'And we mustn't interfere with any of that pagan nonsense, must we?'

'Nonsense?' She was horrified. 'You shouldn't say that, Zak.'

'Oh, come on, Tam!' He was openly scornful. 'The May Day Ritual bringing luck to Luscombe for a year, and all the rest of that rubbish—you surely don't believe it any more?'

But Tamsin shook her head stubbornly. 'I don't know, Zak. What about that time, years ago, when the vicar was so shocked by the Ritual that he made the villagers perform it on the village green instead of out by Luscombe Man, and all the livestock died, and——'

'Oh, for heaven's sake!' Zak roared with laughter. 'Tamsin Westmacott, you really are a superstitious little peasant, after all.' But when she set her mouth in a stubborn line, he said, 'OK, believe it, if you want. Now,' he picked up the serving fork, 'more ham? No? I'll ring for the coffee, then.'

He reached across to press a bellpush by the mantelpiece, and a few moments later the housekeeper appeared with a tray of coffee, a brandy bottle and a plate piled with tiny chocolate-coated choux pastries.

Zak took the tray from her. 'Thanks, Mrs Meadows, I'll see to it. And don't bother to clear away—it's late.'

'Oh, it's no bother, Mr Trenchard.' She gave Tamsin a sidelong look. 'I'll wait till you're finished.'

'No, really,' Zak said firmly. 'There's no need.'

'Very good, sir.' And after an infinitesimal hesitation, 'Goodnight, Tamsin. Goodnight, sir.'

When the door closed, Zak gave a snort of laughter, and Tamsin regarded him uncertainly.

'What's the matter?' she queried.

'Oh—Mrs Meadows. The message coming over loud and clear, in case you didn't realise, was that she's convinced herself that by leaving you alone here in my half of the house she's almost certainly abandoned you to a fate worse than death.'

'Oh, I see.' She tried to speak coolly, but felt the rose-pink tide surge to her cheeks and leaned back quickly, so that her face was shadowed from the revealing glow of the wall lights.

'On the other hand,' Zak slanted her a grin, 'maybe it's all this talk about the Ritual getting to me.'

'What do you mean?'

'Well, after all, it's supposed to be the cleaned-up remnants of an ancient fertility ceremony, isn't it? This business of the dance, for instance.'

'The dance? What about it?'

'Well, in the old days, no doubt, a lot more went on than a quick tango round the village hall. And the Stag King having the first dance with whoever was lucky enough to be his choice as the Maid for that year. Well, I mean...'

He spread his hands in an expressive gesture and, not meeting his eye, Tamsin took a hasty bite of the creamy, feather-light profiterole. Reaching forward, he poured a generous measure of the cognac into a goblet and handed it to her.

'No, none for me, thank you.'

'Nonsense—you need it after getting so chilled out on the moor.'

Zak took up his own glass, swirling the amber liquid around in it, then sipped it thoughtfully. They sat in silence for several minutes, but at last, under cover of lifting her glass, Tamsin risked a surreptitious glance at him.

He was sitting back, his long legs stretched in front of him, and gazing down abstractedly at the carpet. One half of his face, directly illuminated by the glow of firelight, seemed almost boyish; the other half, in deep shadow, retained that tautness about the mouth and jaw which she had come to know so well. Half familiar, half stranger, the man who belonged to the village, just as she did, and yet had grown away from it ...

As she gazed at him, her eyes veiled by her lashes, that painful ache, like a bruise deep inside her, which was becoming so familiar that it almost seemed as much a part of her as breathing, began again. For an instant, her face screwed up as though from a physical blow. Well, it *was* physical, wasn't it? she thought. It was just that the pain-killer for this particular ache hadn't yet been invented.

She realised that Zak was watching her. His face was shadowed now by his arm, bent behind his head, so that she could not make out his expression, but there was something about his stillness that disconcerted her.

'More coffee?' he asked abruptly.

'No, thanks.'

'More brandy, then.' And before she could refuse, he had leaned across to pour the drink.

Instead of sitting back in his chair, though, he came down on his haunches beside her. The firelight was turning his eyes to that strange, pale silver, and Tamsin, after one flickering glance, fixed her gaze on the rim of her glass.

'You know,' he murmured, 'tonight, with your hair down like this, you're——' the faintest smile was playing round his lips '—little Tammy, grown up.'

Her hand moved jerkily, so that the dregs of liquid slopped on to it, and he took the glass from her. Hardly breathing, she willed herself not to react as, taking her wrist, he lowered his head and gently licked up the drops of cognac with his tongue. At the touch of his lips against her skin, though, she felt her pulse quicken treacherously and drew back her hand sharply. But then he was lifting a strand of hair with his finger, holding it so that the fire shone through it, before letting it fall back to her shoulders again.

'Tammy?' he said huskily, and when she looked at him she saw the same expression, a kind of bewildered wonderment, that she had glimpsed in his face that other night.

'Yes, Zak?'

She smiled tremulously up at him, and heard the breath catch in his throat, then, very slowly, he put his hands under her elbows, bringing her forward towards him, and bent over her. His head blotted out the light, his lips all reality beyond the sudden hunger that leapt in her like a dizzying flame to meet the need she sensed in him.

He must have felt her response, for his kiss deepened until his tongue was thrusting far into the deep, secret sweetness of her mouth, his teeth cutting into her soft underlip. One hand went to the back of her head, fastening in her hair to clamp her to him; she felt the other tug impatiently at the knot of her robe and drag it aside, so that it fell from her shoulders.

His warm palm slid in under the hem of the pyjama top, the soft friction of skin against skin setting off tiny explosions of feeling in her nerve-endings. Then the searching fingers were closing on one of her small, firm breasts, and as every pulse in her body cried out he cupped it, his thumb against the rosy nipple, stroking it until it stood erect to meet his touch.

She could feel his other hand ripping open her jacket buttons, and then he bent his head, his lips closing on the throbbing centre of her breast to take it into his mouth. His hand was moving lower now, inside the pyjama trousers, moulding the firm flesh of her buttocks and lifting her into his body. A sound, half sob, half small, throaty gasp of pleasure, was torn out of her, but then, as she hung on the very brink of no return—*Sarah*! The thought flared in her mind and her clenching fingers opened to push him away from her.

'No—*no,* Zak.'

'Tammy,' his voice was ragged, 'don't be a fool. You know you want it as much as I do.'

He reached for her to take her in his arms again but, shuddering, she squirmed out of his grasp, pressing herself into the far corner of the sofa. She began doing up the jacket, but her fingers were still so unsteady that the buttons slipped through them, until Zak gave a muttered exclamation, then, tight-lipped, thrust her hands aside and fastened every button to the neck. Still without a word, he pulled the robe up on to her shoulders and knotted it so tightly that it cut into her ribs, almost as though he was trying to remove all trace of her body from his sight.

Although her head was bent, he must have glimpsed her face, for he swore again, then, pulling her to him, he put his arm round her. He tilted her head gently, took a handkerchief from his pocket and softly dabbed her lip so that she saw the tiny red stain from where his teeth had broken her tender skin.

He jammed the handkerchief back in his pocket, then, still holding her, leaned back against the sofa. There was silence in the room, apart from the dying logs which hissed softly in the grate.

At last he spoke. 'Tammy?'

'Yes?'

'Are you a virgin? You are, aren't you?' he went on, as she gave a violent start.

'Yes.' He had to lean towards her to catch the softly spoken word.

'Well, I suppose I should apologise, then,' he said roughly. 'I'm not usually in the business of plying innocent girls with alcohol and then—despoiling them. And you, of all girls.'

So he hadn't really wanted *her*—little Tammy. Of course, she should have known all along. It had only been the purely physical effect of the brandy and the firelight on a totally masculine body.

'There's no need to apologise, Zak,' she said tightly. 'I quite understand.'

'Do you?' He gave a harsh laugh. 'I'm damned if I do.'

He sat frowning at some point between the chair and the opposite wall for what seemed an endless time, but then finally he broke the silence.

'You know something, Tam? I think you should marry me.'

CHAPTER ELEVEN

'WHAT?' Tamsin jerked upright.

'I said, I think you should marry me.'

As she swivelled round to stare at him, her eyes almost swallowing up the rest of her face, Zak gave her a faint smile. 'Well, say something!'

'But—why?'

He shrugged, rather irritably. 'Oh, because—because—— Do you really need a reason?'

'Well, yes, I do, actually.' Her initial stupefaction was rapidly giving way, under his cool matter-of-factness, to something bordering on crossness.

He pursed his lips. 'OK, then. Let's just say that I think it would be good for both of us.'

'But you——' She broke off, biting her lip. But you don't love me, had teetered on the edge of her tongue, but she wasn't going to grovel for empty reassurances, when she knew all too well what the truth of Zak's feelings for her was.

'No, of course I can't marry you,' she blurted out. And yet wasn't this what she'd dreamed of ever since she could dream?

'Oh, come on, Tam, of course you can.' He put up a finger and gently brushed it across her lips. 'It wouldn't be so painful, would it?'

Yes, it would—it would be anguish, every day of my life. Loving you, and knowing you didn't love me, that you'd only married me—for suddenly she knew that this was the reason—as the only means of getting what you wanted. And yet to be married to Zak—wasn't that one single thing worth all the pain?

'Well?' He was watching her, his face devoid of expression, but she sensed the impatience behind the word.

'Look.' Tamsin traced the tip of her tongue round her lips. 'I can't give you my answer now. You'll have to give me time.'

'I'm not giving you three days this time.' He shot her a meaning look. 'You've got until tomorrow— I'll want my answer at the dance.'

Well, that was all right. She wasn't going to the dance anyway, if he was going to be there, so that would give her a little longer, at least. Slowly she nodded, then gave a huge yawn, not altogether counterfeit.

'If you don't mind, I'd like to go to bed.'

'Mmm.' He studied her critically. 'Yes, you do look all in.'

And before she could protest he had straightened up, scooping her into his arms as though she were a child who had stayed up beyond her bedtime, and was carrying her up the stairs. He nudged open a door with his knee, went in and set her down on the carpet.

As he flicked on the bedside lights, Tamsin's eyes took in the room. It was attractively furnished, with light modern wood, and pretty floral curtains and matching quilt. By the window was a lovely little tub chair in pink velvet, and draped across it were her clothes, washed, dried and ironed. It was warm in here already, but Zak switched on the wall-mounted gas fire, then indicated another door.

'Your bathroom's through there.' He put a hand on the bed. 'Good, Mrs Meadows has put the electric blanket on. If you want anything,' he turned to face her, or, at least, not quite to face her—their eyes scarcely met, 'my room's at the far end of the corridor.'

He paused and took half a step towards her, so that for a moment she thought he was going to kiss her. But then he stopped, said an abrupt, 'Good-night, Tammy,' and before she could mumble a reply he had gone.

Straining her ears, she stood listening while he went along the corridor, then a door opened and closed. Restlessly she began pacing up and down, hugging her arms to her chest, but then, as one of the old floorboards creaked loudly under her foot, she froze, terrified that he might have heard her moving about and be coming back. When nothing happened, though, she crept silently across the room, switched off the blanket and slid under the quilt.

She closed her eyes resolutely, but for a long time sleep stubbornly refused to come. Finally, though, she drifted into an uneasy half-doze, filled with disturbing dreams and images, until as, for the twentieth time, she fell towards that swirling torrent of water at her feet, she gave a smothered cry and jerked into consciousness.

Pale daylight was filtering through a tiny gap in the curtains and she got out of bed, slipped on her robe, and crossed to the window. She half drew the curtains and perched on the wide sill. At one side of the lawn was a blue and white striped marquee— the refreshment tent for the dance, probably. If she said yes to Zak, he would dance with her all night down there. Maybe—no, certainly—he'd announce their engagement, and the whole village would be so glad for her...

Just what was it that had provoked Zak's proposal? It must have been that brief, abortive scene by the fire. Tamsin groaned aloud at the shaming memory and laid her hot forehead against the cool glass. The one thing for her to be grateful for was that she'd been strong enough to resist him, otherwise by now they would have become lovers.

Just like him and Sarah. The thought leapt into her mind. Sarah. She didn't want to think of her friend, but suddenly she was all around her. Maybe that was why Zak had begun to make love to her— he'd certainly been more than half angry with himself, right from the beginning. Perhaps he secretly regretted his abandonment of Sarah and down there, in the firelight, she'd somehow reminded him of her. But she didn't want to be a substitute Sarah—she'd lived in her shadow for long enough.

In any case, perhaps it was all more cynical than that. Had he so readily broken off his lovemaking, calculating that this would only make her all the more eager to accept his proposal? After all, that technique, or something very like it—with its sweet-talk of marriage—had worked well enough with one girl, hadn't it, so why not with the other? The only difference was that in her case, it seemed as if Zak actually intended marriage—a fair price to pay for Wethertor, to his twisted way of thinking.

No. However much she might still yearn for him, a loveless marriage was, for her, too high a price to pay. And yet she shrank back from the thought of facing him. She could at least take these few hours' respite he'd given her.

Leaping to her feet, she dragged off his robe and pyjamas and without even bothering to wash her face pulled on her own clothes. As she turned to go, she looked down on to the lawn again and just for a moment longer allowed herself to keep the image—herself held close in Zak's arms, her head against his chest, as they danced the last slow waltz—then she turned away.

Every stair tread creaked and she held her breath, but the house remained silent. In the hall, she hesitated. Joss. Should she leave him—ask Matt to collect him later—or take the risk of Zak hearing them both? As she gnawed her underlip in indecision, a faint noise came from overhead and she flew to the front door, slid back the bolts and let herself out.

Matt was in the yard, his bicycle propped against the stable.

'Morning, Tamsin. You all right now?'

'Yes, thanks, I'm fine.'

'Well, I knew Mr Trenchard would take good care of you. But there was no need for you to hurry back—I've done everything that needs seeing to.'

On an impulse, Tamsin stretched up and kissed the old man's sunburnt face. 'Thanks, Matt. What would I do without you?'

'Oh, go along with you.' He shuffled his shoulders in embarrassment. 'Anyway, I'll be getting off now—got to pick up my fiddle and smock. So I'll see you later.'

'Oh, well, I'm not really sure,' she began lamely, but he had turned away and didn't hear her.

And after all, she might as well go to the May Ritual—in fact, it would probably be as well if she did. With her disappearing at five in the morning, Zak might well arrive on the doorstep at any moment, demanding to know what the hell she was up to. And at the Ritual there would at least be safety in numbers—he could hardly pounce on her with all of Luscombe looking on.

Indoors, she made herself a cup of tea and some toast, then, having locked the front door so that no one could take her unawares, she went upstairs, showered and took out the dress which she'd worn to every Ritual since she was thirteen. Made from Sarah's mother's white silk wedding dress, it had been first for Sarah, but when she grew tall and well developed, Mrs Warren had passed it on to the much smaller Tamsin.

She lifted it out of the old sheet in which it was carefully stored and stepped into it, pulling it up around her, zipping it, then finally turned to survey herself in the mirror. The dress fell in pale, pearly folds to her ankles, the long tight sleeves and high, severe neckline emphasising her slender fragility. She'd lost weight since last year, and her face was thinner; her eyes, shadowed by the wistfulness so often evident in them, looked enormous.

As she smoothed out the folds of the skirt, she saw near the waist the tiny, beautifully mended tear. She stared at it. She'd been—what?—fourteen. At the dance, Zak, even more exuberant than usual, had been swinging her round in his unique version of the samba when the buckle of his jeans had caught in her waistband. 'It's all right,' she'd told him. 'Easily mended.' More easily than hearts...

She put on her white sandals, picked up her grandmother's lovely old Paisley shawl, and went downstairs.

Most of the villagers were already there, milling around on the grass and dwarfed by the towering granite column of Luscombe Man. Tamsin moved among them, greeting and being greeted by the people she had known all her life, and finally joined the group of girls and young women who were clustered together near the stone, all in their traditional white dresses.

Together they stood and watched as the vicar's wife, looking even more harassed than usual, shepherded her reluctant flock of Sunday School children to a roped-off section of grass and lined them up. One of the fathers struck a ringing chord from his accordion and launched headlong into 'Follow my Lover'.

But while everyone else's attention was riveted on the solemn-faced children performing one country dance after another, Tamsin's eyes were searching feverishly among the crowd. Zak, though, was not there. Probably he'd outgrown the Ritual, as he'd outgrown everything else—pagan non-sense, he'd called it, hadn't he? So, gradually, she relaxed enough to enjoy the familiar pattern of music and weaving dance shapes.

The applause died away and the crowd gradually fell silent as, from beyond the hilltop, there came the faint sound of music. Then the Luscombe Morris Men appeared, led by Matt in his grand-father's beautifully embroidered shepherd's smock, playing that strange, rather eerie little tune on his violin that, however many times she heard it, made the hair on Tamsin's neck stand on end. And then, behind them, cresting the ridge, came the Stag King.

The canvas-skirted costume hung in the church between Rituals, as though to nullify its pagan in-fluence, but ever since she was a child Tamsin had never been able to go into the vestry without a shiver at the sight of that shapeless shape, hanging from a peg in the corner, the huge, antlered head staring down at her. Now, reared up, with a man inside, it was even more menacing as it pranced between the two rows of dancers.

'He's good this year, isn't he?' Tamsin said to the girl beside her.

'Well, Joanne certainly thinks so.' The other girl smiled and they exchanged knowing looks.

So the Stag King this year was Darren Yeates, Joanne's fiancé. By tradition, the identity of the villager playing the part—a different man each year—was kept secret, but everyone always knew, just as it was also an open secret that the Stag would choose his sweetheart as his Maid.

Matt's playing became shriller, more insistent, as from among the Morris Men stepped the figure of St George, complete with sword and shield. Gradually the group weaved inwards, forming a tighter and tighter knot around the Stag, until only the magnificent head and shoulders were visible. Then the rest moved back, St George leapt forward and, as the familiar half-fear, half-exultation clutched at Tamsin's throat, he struck down the beast. Standing over it, he raised the wooden sword, which five thousand years ago would no doubt have been a real weapon, and, as the onlookers breathed a faint, involuntary sigh, gave the final death blow. The Stag quivered, fell, rolled over and over, and finally lay still.

'He's really great, Joanne.' Tamsin had to shout above the applause. Darren had excelled himself; never until now had he struck her as having much more natural acting ability than one of her ewes.

'Now, girls, off you go!'

Mrs Davies began chivvying them all towards the standing stone and, suppressing nervous giggles, they formed a large circle round it, Tamsin finding herself between Joanne and her younger sister. When the Stag, now miraculously restored to life, leapt into the centre of the ring, they all joined hands and, as Matt's playing changed to a slower, more sensuous rhythm, began circling it.

Round and round the great beast pranced, making threatening runs at each of the girls in turn, and, with Luscombe Man towering behind it, Tamsin was suddenly reminded of one of those primitive animal cave paintings, drawn to bring luck in hunting—only in this case the Stag was the hunter, not the hunted.

All at once it advanced on her, the huge head lowered as though to charge, and she ducked away, laughing. But then, moments later, as she came within range again, the Stag bore down on her once more and this time the canvas folds parted and she was dragged inside, fetching up hard against a masculine body. Trapped in the enveloping folds, she struggled wildly.

'Stop it, Darren, you idiot,' she gasped. 'You've got the wrong one. I'm not——'

'For God's sake, Tammy,' the voice came from the darkness, 'stop flinging yourself around or you'll have us both over!'

Horrified, she stilled instantly. 'Let me go.'

'Certainly not.' Zak put his arms round her, clasping her to him and, lifting her clean off her feet, whirled her round with him.

'Put me down, will you?'

It was almost impossible to breathe, and besides, she was jammed up so close against Zak that she was dreadfully conscious of every contour of his body. And yet, even here in this smothering darkness, it was bliss just to be held securely in his arms, and she knew suddenly that of every place on earth this was where she wanted to be——

'Oh, come on, Tammy. Relax—enjoy it.'

In the dim, greenish light, she could just make out the white gleam of his teeth. He was laughing at her; it was just a joke to him.

'No, I won't, damn you!'

Struggling free, she dug the point of her elbow hard into his midriff; he gave a grunt and loosed his hold on her. They teetered dangerously for a moment and almost fell, but then Tamsin clawed her way out of the stiff canvas folds and emerged, to hear all round her the cheers and raucous laughter.

Her hair was all over her face; as she brushed it aside she saw that her skirt had ridden up round her thighs. Scarlet-faced, she tugged it down, then, unable to face those teasing smiles, she fled.

He came, as she'd known he would. Resisting the pointless impulse to turn and run yet again, she watched as he strode along the woodland path, ducking his tall figure beneath the overhanging trees.

He surveyed her in silence, then, 'Why ever did you run away?' But his voice was gentle.

'Don't know.' Tamsin shrugged, and to try to cover her tension she picked up a couple of mossy pebbles and tossed them into the stream.

'I gather you didn't appreciate my little surprise?'

'Not really.' Her voice wobbled slightly. 'I think I must have lost my sense of humour, or something.'

'Oh, Tam.' Zak dropped down beside her. 'I'm sorry if I upset you, but Mrs Davies lumbered me with the job last night. That fool Darren put his back out falling off his motorbike and she was desperate. I nearly told you after she rang, but it's supposed to be a secret, and then when I saw you this morning—well, I couldn't resist grabbing you.'

He gave her a sideways smile, but when she did not respond, he went on enticingly. 'You must admit I was pretty good. Matt swears I was the best Stag King ever.'

'Yes, well, Matt always was a push-over,' she muttered ungraciously, but he refused to be put off.

'And anyway, it seemed the best way of ensuring that you have the first dance with me tonight.'

'I'm not going to the dance, Zak.' Tamsin was gazing fixedly at a clump of late primroses on the opposite bank.

'Why not?'

'For the same reason that I—left the Manor this morning.' Now she turned and looked steadily at him. 'There's no need for you to wait till tonight for your answer, Zak. I shan't marry you.'

'Any particular reason?'

'Because—because you don't love me.'

'I see,' he said slowly. 'Well, I suppose I can't exactly blame you for thinking that—when I couldn't even see it for myself.'

Was it his words, or the expression in his eyes, that was beginning to make her insides flutter madly?

'No, Tam, I just couldn't make that quantum leap. I couldn't follow you,' he went on, as she looked at him in puzzlement, 'from being the irritating, exasperating, infuriating little kid, who was as familiar to me as—as myself, to being the irritating, exasperating, pain-in-the-backside, lovely, desirable young woman you've become.'

Her head was lowered now, but very gently he put his thumb under her chin, turning her face to his, so that there was nowhere else for her to look but at him.

'Every time I saw you, I had this strange feeling, at one and the same time wanting to shake the life out of you, and to snatch you up into my arms. Even yesterday, when I saw you huddled on that rock, and in the middle of my terror for you I suddenly realised with a blinding flash that my life could never be quite the same without you, I still didn't get the message.'

He shot her a rueful smile. 'Last night, I think my body finally got tired of waiting for my pea-sized brain to fathom what had happened to me and it said, in no uncertain terms, "Move over, moron, and let me show you exactly what I want." And then, when you broke free from me, it finally dawned on me that——'

As he stopped, Tamsin hardly dared breathe. 'That——?'

'That I love you, that I adore you—that I want to stand on tiptoe and shout it to the whole world. Marry me, Tammy—or I shall go crazy, I think.' He seized her by the shoulders, holding her so that she could not move, then demanded tensely, 'Well?'

'Oh, Zak.' She gave him the softest of smiles, but then, with a sick lurch of her stomach, she knew her answer. 'No—I can't.'

'Why?' He shook her roughly. 'You believe me, don't you?'

'Yes, Zak, I do. But—Sarah.' She could scarcely get the word out.

'Sarah?' He stared at her blankly. 'But why should she stop you?'

Why? He still couldn't see. She felt the jags of ice settle round her heart again, and drew herself back from him.

'Look, Tammy.' His voice was urgent. 'I know how much Sarah meant to you, but you can't spend the rest of your life mourning her. She wouldn't want you to, believe me.'

'No, I dare say not. But if you think I could marry the man who broke her heart——'

'What? What the hell are you talking about?'

'You and Sarah, of course,' she said wearily, and, gathering her skirts around her, made to get up.

But he snatched her by the wrist, dragging her back down. 'Tell me what you mean, Tam.' His voice was dangerously quiet.

'All right, if I really have to spell it out for you,' she said flatly. 'You were lovers. You promised to marry her, then you went away, just like that,' she snapped her fingers, 'and left her without a word. She was heartbroken, Zak.' But all her anger had gone; she only felt pain and grief.

'Look at me.' When she still stared down at her lap, he grabbed her by the arms and shook her violently. 'Look at me, damn you! Sarah and I were never lovers. *Never.*'

Two angry circles of crimson blazed in her cheeks. 'Of course you were. She told me——'

'On my solemn honour, Tamsin,' his level glance dared her to interrupt him, 'we were never lovers. I never regarded her in any way other than—well, as a girl I'd known all my life.'

'But—but that night you went away——' She broke off, bewildered yet still fiercely loyal to her friend.

'Surely you knew that Sarah was a dreamer?' he demanded. 'She was a lovely girl, but she didn't live in the real world—she lived in fantasies, where she was always the heroine. I don't know what stories she fed you——'

He in turn broke off, biting his lip, but Tamsin stared up at him. He was right—she knew that now. So close to Sarah herself, she hadn't been able to see it, and yet—even on the morning of the wedding, that scene in the kitchen, there had been something unnatural about her, as though she were acting a part for an unseen audience. And yet——

'But you stopped me going out with both of you.' In spite of the years, something of the pain she'd felt at being pushed away came through in her voice. 'You told Sarah that you wanted to go out riding just with her.'

'What?' Zak stared at her, but then a strange expression came down over his face, like a shutter. 'Yes, well—you always were a little pest, weren't you?'

But he wasn't meeting her eye squarely.

'It wasn't true, was it?' she said slowly, her voice quivering. 'Not wanting me with you any more. It wasn't you—it was Sarah, wasn't it?'

'Oh, my darling.' At the desolation in her tone, Zak pulled her into his arms and held her slim little body tightly to him, waiting for the tremors that rocked it to ease.

When finally they did, he shifted his grip on her slightly, tilting her face to his, and as they stared at one another, scarcely breathing, the air between them seemed to shimmer as if with tiny particles of electricity.

'Oh, my love,' said Zak shakily, and, catching a strand of her hair which was falling across her face, he tucked it behind her ear, then, bending forward, kissed her full on the lips.

She kissed him back, straining her body to his, in an endless embrace, but at last his mouth left hers, sliding down her throat to the pulse at the base. She felt her blood quicken, here and in all the other pulse-points of her body, and Zak must have felt it too, for his grasp tightened, then his fingers slid behind her shoulders to unfasten the waist-length zip of her dress.

Slowly he drew it down, peeling her arms from the long, tight sleeves, to reveal the rounded curves of her breasts above her lacy bra. With slightly shaking hands, he undid the catch to lift it from her, then sat back on his heels, gazing at her. Looking down, she saw her own body, naked to the hips, in a pool of white silk.

When her glance flickered to him he was watching her, his eyes rapt although he made no effort to touch her, and at the intensity of his expression she was filled fleetingly with a trembling shyness.

But then she put this feeling from her; she was a woman and Zak loved her, desired her. She put out her hand to him, just as he reached towards her. Their palms met, held, then he pulled her to him, lifting her up to draw the dress from her, then shedding his own clothes as she clung to him.

He laid her down on the mossy grass, the sunlight filtering through the trees overhead and the points of light from the stream dappling their bodies, so that they looked like underwater creatures of green and black and gold.

'Oh, Tammy,' his voice shook, 'you're so beautiful.'

She wasn't—and yet, maybe, today, loved by Zak, she had become beautiful.

Propped on his elbow, he ran his fingers down the length of her body, over her breasts, down across her flat stomach and the slight curve of her hip to the soft flesh of her inner thigh, so that she gasped with shocked pleasure.

But still she sensed that he was holding himself back from her. Rather uncertainly, she put out her hand and stroked his chest, feeling the silky black hairs and the small nipples, which tightened under her thumb. Then, emboldened, she moved her hand down, delighting in the feel of the taut stomach muscles, and lower——

'No, don't.' It was almost a groan. 'I won't——'

'Shh.' She laid a finger on his lips. 'Please, Zak.' And she put her arms around him, drawing him down to her.

'Tammy—no. Not yet.'

'*Yes*.' Then, as he surrendered and moved across her, 'Oh, yes!'

But still he entered her with tender compassion, pausing as she gave a tiny gasp against his chest and clenched her hands on his shoulders to drop baby kisses on her brow and closed eyelids, and make soothing murmurs against her mouth, until she relaxed under him.

When he began to move, she felt his rhythm take hold of her, building within her, slowly at first, then, as pleasure so exquisite that it was almost pain washed through her, she was caught up in that insistent rhythm and carried along by it, like a river plunging headlong to meet the sea.

She ceased altogether to be flesh and blood and was pure sensation, until finally, when the feeling was almost too much for her to bear, the river joined the sea in a surge of spray, a roar like thunder in her ears, and she was flung down, broken and dying, on the shore . . .

'Tammy?'

She stirred and, miraculously still alive, opened her eyes to see Zak looking down at her. The hard lines of his face were softened and a tender smile hovered round his mouth. Reaching across her, he snapped off a flower stem, brushed it sensuously across her lips, then slid it into a silky tendril of hair.

'A flower for the Stag King's nymph.' And the look he gave her made her melt inside. But then he tapped the end of her nose. 'Time to go.'

'Oh, but I want to stay here all day.'

But when she yawned and stretched her body languorously, he shook his head firmly. 'No, I'm taking you back home. I left Joss pacing up and down the hall, utterly convinced that something terrible had happened to you.'

'Well,' she gave him a slow smile, 'something terrible *has* happened, hasn't it? It's not every day that a wood nymph is pounced on by the Stag King.'

'Don't remind me.' Zak shifted his shoulders. 'That costume was quite a weight. And with a decidedly unwilling Maid to contend with—well!' He rolled his eyes expressively, but then the laughter in them faded. 'In any case, I want to take you down to Torbay this afternoon.'

She tensed. 'Oh? You mean——?'

'Yes. To meet my father.' He was not quite looking at her now. 'He's very anxious to make his peace with you.'

Just for a moment Tamsin hesitated, but then she smiled up at him. 'Yes, of course, Zak. I'll be happy to meet him.'

As she smoothed back her hair to something like order, the flower that he had tucked into it tumbled on to her lap. She stared at it, then clapped her hand to her mouth with a gasp of horror.

'Oh, no—he'll go mad!'

'Who will? What's the matter?' Zak was looking at her as though she were ever so slightly moonstruck.

'Brian.' She rolled over, then, regardless of her nakedness, leapt to her feet. 'Oh, God—we've been lying all over them!' she wailed. 'He'll think I've done it on purpose and I'll end up in prison—or something dreadful.'

As a giggle of nervous terror welled up in her, she caught Zak's eye. 'These——' she gestured towards the crushed orchids '—they're Summer Lady's Tresses.'

'So? What about them?'

'They're very rare—practically extinct. These certainly are now,' she added mournfully, surveying the spot where they'd lain.

'Well, there are plenty more all along the stream there. Brian, whoever he is, won't miss these few.'

'Oh!' For the second time Tamsin clapped her hand to her mouth and sank down, looking at him, her eyes round with guilt. 'I meant to tell you, but

I forgot. I can't use the wood any more—they're going to put a protection order on it.'

'What? No more war games?'

'Not in the wood—no.'

'Hmm.' He was frowning. 'That puts a different complexion on things. If I can't use the wood——'

'It—it doesn't make any difference, does it, Zak?' The tiniest seed of doubt was sprouting in her mind.

'Well,' he said doubtfully, 'I'm not sure——' But then, as the laughter burst from him, he pulled her to him. 'Oh, my darling Tammy, I mustn't tease you any more. Of course it doesn't—I wouldn't care if there were a hundred protection orders slapped on this place. And anyway, we'll either work the games round it—or maybe helicopter the teams over it. That'll give them even more of a thrill.'

'So you still want to go ahead and marry me— even without my precious wood?' She was able now to shoot him a sidelong, mischievous look.

'Just you try and stop me.'

He picked up the orchid she had discarded, and as she knelt above him he traced it in a delicate pattern around her navel, then tossed it away and drew her to him once more.

CHAPTER TWELVE

JUST as Tamsin turned over, Zak surfaced in the pool beside her, tossing the water back from his hair. Pulling her into his arms, he kissed her, their wet, suntanned limbs twining in the water, deep turquoise in the glow from the underwater lights.

'Out you get. It's nearly time to dress for dinner.'

'Oh, no.' Tamsin protested. 'Just two more lengths.'

'*No.*' He dropped a kiss on the tip of her nose, then towed her, still protesting, to the wide shallow steps at the far end of the pool. 'Out!'

He gave her bottom a light smack to help her on her way and she hauled herself out, then picked up her beach towel from the padded lounger and began blotting herself dry.

'Here, let me help you.'

Zak, a white towel draped round his gleaming, bronzed shoulders, took it from her and, as she lifted her wet hair out of the way, dried her back.

'Ouch!' She eased the straps of her pink bikini from her shoulders. 'I've caught the sun, I think.'

He scowled. 'You never do as you're told, do you? I tried to make you lie under that thatched beach shade this morning.'

'And leave you to those two girls who were so busy chatting you up? Not likely.' She gave him a mock-severe look as he helped her into her white towelling robe, but he gave a snort of laughter.

'You needn't have worried. I've always made a point of not flirting with other women while I'm on my honeymoon. Besides, they're not my type.'

'Oh, and what is your type, then?'

But his look answered the question for her. He gave his hair and chest a perfunctory rub with the towel, then, arms linked, they strolled back through the swathe of palms and sweetly perfumed shrubs that divided the pool from the low-set thatched bungalows that, spread among the jacaranda trees, formed the hotel complex.

On the steps to their bungalow they halted and stood, drinking in the sights and scents, as all round them the warm African twilight deepened from azure to violet to indigo and from beyond the line of palms came the insistent shush-shush of the Indian Ocean lapping on to the powdery white sand.

Tamsin, her head cushioned against Zak's shoulder, gave a blissful sigh. 'Oh, it's like a dream, isn't it? I keep thinking, if I pinch myself hard enough I'll wake up.'

He rumpled her hair. 'No dream—unless I'm sharing the identical one.'

'No, you're right. It isn't.' She held up her left hand, with its wide, plain band of dark gold on her third finger, then gave him a rather shy-eyed smile. 'I couldn't have imagined *this*.'

'And now you know why I didn't get your engagement ring before we left.'

'Mmm. I thought, with everything being ar-
ranged in such a rush——' she still felt faintly
breathless when she remembered the speed and
smooth efficiency with which Zak had had her
walking down the aisle of the village church '—that
you'd forgotten.'

'And you really do like my choice? I saw the em-
eralds when I was out here in Mombasa last year,
but didn't think then that I'd be sliding one of them
on to your finger.'

As she held up her hand, the beautiful rough-cut
stone sent out flashes of ice-cold fire, reflected from
the lights behind them.

'Yes, it's wonderful. Thank you, Zak,' she said
softly.

'My pleasure.'

He plucked a pink hibiscus flower from the bush
beside them and tucked it into her bikini top, so
that its silky petals brushed against her breasts.

'And thank you for saying we'll live at the farm.'

He shrugged. 'Oh, I know how much the old
place means to you—far more than the Manor
means to me. All the same, how do you fancy
staying on here for another week? We can, if you
want.'

'Oh no, Zak,' she said quickly. 'I know you have
to get back.'

'Although you, of course,' he flashed her a
teasing smile, 'wouldn't care if you never saw your
precious Wethertor again.'

'Well,' she smiled rather shamefacedly, 'I have
been wondering how Matt's getting on—and Joss,

of course.' She paused. 'You really meant it—that I needn't send the sheep to market?'

'Of course—they can all live to a happy old age. Although I shall be the laughing stock of the county, you realise that? "Zak Trenchard? Oh, he's gone soft in the head over that young wife of his."'

'Yes, but—I didn't tell you—I've had this marvellous idea about going organic. It's all the rage now. People are willing to pay for vegetables with no pesticides and——'

'All right, all right—and I've had this marvellous idea about how that upstairs room would make a perfect nursery, so don't go making too many plans for the farm.'

'Oh.' Tamsin felt the colour rising to her cheeks. 'I——'

But she was silenced by Zak's mouth and only emerged, breathless and weak-kneed from his kiss, a long time later. He picked her up, carried her across the veranda and through the sitting-room, to toss her down on the bed.

'Zak, no!' Laughing, she scrambled to her feet. 'You said it's time to dress for dinner.'

'Uh-uh.' He shook his head, his eyes gleaming in the half-light. 'I said it was *nearly* time to dress for dinner.'

Reaching out, he unknotted her wrap and pulled her clear of it. Unhooking her top, he slid it away from her damp skin to reveal her small, rounded breasts, then kneeling in front of her he drew down her bikini pants. He straightened up and stood surveying her, drinking in her body.

'My lovely, perfect little naiad with the sea-green eyes.'

And, reflected in the long mirror behind him, she saw a slender young woman, all soft curves and satin skin, with long fair hair on her shoulders, and wide, dark green eyes. She gave that new self a shy smile. Lovely? Yes, loving Zak—or rather, being loved by him—really had worked this magic.

'My darling, you know something?' Zak's lips curved in a tender smile. 'I think I've been waiting all your life for you to grow up into—this.'

The palms rustled outside, a silver moon rose from the ocean, as she held out her arms to him and gave him a slow, sensuous little smile.

'Well, then,' she said simply, 'here I am.'

BARBARY WHARF

**An exciting six-book series, one title per month
beginning in October, by bestselling author**

Charlotte Lamb

Set in the glamorous and fast-paced world of international
journalism, BARBARY WHARF will take you from the
Sentinel's hectic newsroom to the most thrilling cities in the
world. You'll meet media tycoon Nick Caspian and his
adversary Gina Tyrrell, whose dramatic story of passion and
heartache develops throughout the six-book series.

In book one, BESIEGED (#1498), you'll also meet Hazel and
Piet. Hazel's always had a good word to say about everyone.
Well, almost. She just can't stand Piet Van Leyden, Nick's
chief architect and one of the most arrogant know-it-alls she's
ever met! As far as Hazel's concerned, Piet's a twentieth-
century warrior, and she's the one being besieged!

Don't miss the sparks in the first BARBARY WHARF
book, BESIEGED (#1498), available in October from
Harlequin Presents.

BARB-S

JAYNE ANN KRENTZ

A two-part epic tale from one of today's most popular romance novelists!

Dreams
Parts One & Two

The warrior died at her feet, his blood running out of the cave entrance and mingling with the waterfall. With his last breath he cursed the woman—told her that her spirit would remain chained in the cave forever until a child was created and born there....

So goes the ancient legend of the Chained Lady and the curse that bound her throughout the ages—until destiny brought Diana Prentice and Colby Savager together under the influence of forces beyond their understanding. Suddenly they were both haunted by dreams that linked past and present, while their waking hours were filled with danger. Only when Colby, Diana's modern-day warrior, learned to love, could those dark forces be vanquished. Only then could Diana set the Chained Lady free....

**Available in September
wherever Harlequin books are sold.**

JK92

HARLEQUIN
Romance®

HARLEQUIN ROMANCE IS BETTING ON LOVE!

And The Bridal Collection's September title is a sure bet.

JACK OF HEARTS (#3218) by Heather Allison

THE BRIDAL COLLECTION

THE BRIDE played her part.
THE GROOM played for keeps.
THEIR WEDDING was in the cards!

Available in August in
THE BRIDAL COLLECTION:

THE BEST-MADE PLANS (#3214) by Leigh Michaels

Harlequin Romance

Wherever Harlequin books are sold.

WED-5

Take 4 bestselling love stories FREE

Plus get a FREE surprise gift!

Special Limited-time Offer

Mail to Harlequin Reader Service®

In the U.S.	In Canada
3010 Walden Avenue	P.O. Box 609
P.O. Box 1867	Fort Erie, Ontario
Buffalo, N.Y. 14269-1867	L2A 5X3

YES! Please send me 4 free Harlequin Presents® novels and my free surprise gift. Then send me 6 brand-new novels every month, which I will receive months before they appear in bookstores. Bill me at the low price of $2.49* each—a savings of 40¢ apiece off the cover prices. There are no shipping, handling or other hidden costs. I understand that accepting the books and gift places me under no obligation ever to buy any books. I can always return a shipment and cancel at any time. Even if I never buy another book from Harlequin, the 4 free books and the surprise gift are mine to keep forever.

*Offer slightly different in Canada—$2.49 per book plus 69¢ per shipment for delivery. Canadian residents add applicable federal and provincial sales tax. Sales tax applicable in N.Y.

106 BPA ADLZ   306 BPA ADMF

Name _____ (PLEASE PRINT)

Address _____ Apt. No. _____

City _____ State/Prov. _____ Zip/Postal Code _____

This offer is limited to one order per household and not valid to present Harlequin Presents® subscribers. Terms and prices are subject to change.

PRES-92   © 1990 Harlequin Enterprises Limited